SOMETHING GAINED

(or the winning of a very sensible girl)

ELISABETH C. THOMPSON

E.T. Thompson

ATLANTIS PUBLICATIONS

© Elisabeth C. Thompson 2008
Something Gained

ISBN : 978-0-9556971-1-1

Published by
Atlantis Publications
11, Guildford Place
Chichester
West Sussex
PO19 5DU

A CIP catalogue record of this book
can be obtained from the British Library.

Designed & produced by Michael Walsh at
THE BETTER BOOK COMPANY

a division of
RPM Print & Design
2-3 Spur Road
Chichester
West Sussex
PO19 8PR

*For my two dogs, Darcey and Winnie
and for my mother, Betty,
who has patiently and stoically
read every word I have written.*

1

Isobel awoke to the sound of her two puppies scrapping over a bone. She smiled to herself and turned her head to glance at the alarm clock which told her that it was already past seven o'clock.

She rolled over to look across at her husband Adrian, still sleeping peacefully beside her in their elegant four-poster bed and wondered lazily to herself why she seemed so keen to be up and about on a Saturday morning … and then it came to her. She remembered that today was the day their daughter Pippa was arriving to pay them a very welcome visit.

Pippa was staying at a nearby hotel and had travelled up to Cumbria from her home in the South of England the previous day. Her career as an auctioneer in Linchester did not leave her much time to make trips up north at the drop of a hat and Isobel was delighted that she was coming this weekend and even more pleased that she was not coming alone. Pippa would be bringing Ian with her, the new man in her life. The prospect of meeting the someone special in Pippa's life really excited Isobel, incurable romantic that she was. Pippa would be celebrating her thirty-eighth birthday in September and in her mother's opinion, it was high time she was married.

In her mind's eye, Isobel started to see a big wedding. Pippa in a gorgeous dress, several bridesmaids processing down the aisle behind her and rose petals showering down over the happy couple. She could almost hear the music and smell the flowers decorating the little country church in the village. Then, after that, grandchildren started arriving in her dream world; three, or was that four?

The grandfather clock in the hall struck the half-hour dragging Isobel reluctantly back from the land of make-believe. She slid out of bed feet first trying not to disturb her supine husband, tucked her toes into two fluffy white slippers and, carefully unhitching her dressing gown from the back of the bedroom door, she slipped it over her shoulders and left the room silently, closing the door carefully behind her.

Adrian snored loudly and turned over in bed, but he was still fast asleep as she crept downstairs to be greeted by ecstatic yelping from Nip and Tuck, her two lively Lakeland Terriers.

Having let the dogs out and checked for accidents (because although they were now twelve months old and house-trained, the pleasure of seeing their mistress after a whole night's absence was almost too much for their self-control) Isobel put the kettle on to boil for her first cup of coffee of the morning. Then she fed the dogs and sat down to drink her coffee.

The puppies, having wolfed down their food, were now trying to chew her slippers and she pushed them away gently several times, finally giving up the unequal struggle and putting her feet up on a chair instead, while she thought about her daughter's imminent visit.

As she sipped her coffee, she wondered what Ian looked like. Pippa had joked that he was tall, dark and handsome, but that could mean anything. From what she had gleaned from another of her daughter's recent telephone calls, Ian's mother had unfortunately died within the last few months and as if that had not been enough to deal with, he had apparently also been made redundant, poor man. Reading between the lines, she had the impression that Pippa was rather taken with Ian and he sounded like a very nice person, but she would just have to wait and see what she thought when she met him. Isobel made a point of never making up her mind about people until she met them face to face and she knew that her daughter had inherited her good judgment where people were concerned so she was not worried about Pippa's new boyfriend at all, in fact she was really looking forward to meeting him.

The central heating boiler growled into action and Isobel, seeing steam coming out of the kettle again, took it off the Aga and went to make Adrian his early morning cup of tea. She did not know exactly what time to expect Pippa, but she wanted them both to be ready in good time.

"Wake up, sleepy-head!"

Adrian slowly came to and focused on his wife who was smiling down on him. He smiled back.

"Morning darling."

"I've brought you a cup of tea and now I'm going to have a quick shower," said Isobel putting the cup and saucer down carefully on the small table beside the bed.

"What's the rush?" he asked, still half asleep. "It can't be more than eight o'clock."

"Don't tell me you have forgotten already darling, Pippa is coming for lunch," she said patiently, as she walked off into the bathroom, leaving him to wake up properly.

Adrian sat up in bed and felt for his glasses on the bedside table. When the bedroom came into focus, he located his cup of tea and took a sip. Yes, he *did* remember, Pippa was coming to see them and bringing a bloke with her. It would be good to have some male company for a change, he mused. He was usually in a minority of one when she came to visit, as even the dogs were female. Hadn't Pippa explained that he was an engineer? He should be quite sensible then Adrian decided with some satisfaction, remembering back to some of Pippa's other conquests who had left him despairing of the younger generation. He switched on the radio to hear the news and made up his mind to get up when Isobel had finished in the bathroom; in the meantime he reckoned he could enjoy his tea in peace.

Not a million miles away, the subject of his mental meanderings was sitting at a table for two in the dining room of the Killingbeck Ridge Hotel, tucking into a hearty English breakfast, opposite Adrian's daughter, Pippa, who was doing likewise. Ian had booked the hotel over the Internet and was very relieved to find that it had easily exceeded his expectations. The three-course meal the previous evening had been superb, from the grilled goat's cheese starter through the carefully prepared duck right up to the last mouthful of lemon syllabub and this morning's breakfast had not disappointed either.

Their room was comfortable and newly decorated and the staff were very friendly and helpful, so all in all the hotel had been a very lucky find he thought to himself.

"More coffee Ian?" Pippa asked politely, holding up the cafetière.

"Yes, please. That was a delicious sausage. I don't think I could eat another thing," declared Ian happily.

"Do you feel like a walk down to the lake then? We couldn't see anything last night, and I really want to show you how lovely it is here. Actually it's still a bit misty, but with a bit of luck that will clear later," she said, glancing out of the dining room windows which, unlike those at the front of the hotel that boasted a superb view of the lake, overlooked farmland stretching almost as far as the eye could see; swathes of green broken only by the long grey snakes of dry stone walling and punctuated by a solitary tree here and there, all of it encompassed by the misty mauve of the fells beyond.

"I think a walk is just what I need," said Ian with a laugh, stretching and getting up from the table. "How far is it?"

"Probably about a mile, but we will need our coats," said Pippa sensibly as she followed him out into the hall.

Isobel brushed her long burnished locks and looked at herself in the mirror. Her lively green eyes peered back at her a little short-sightedly as she checked her appearance and then she pulled a face as she scrutinised her laughter lines a little more closely. She remembered once being told by her grandmother that by the time you had reached a certain age, you were left with the face you deserved. Well, hers was not too bad for nearly sixty-three and at least her hair hadn't fallen out yet; it had kept most of its colour too she noted with pride. With one deft movement Isobel knotted her hair into a bun at the nape of her neck, tweaked it a bit here and there and then finally satisfied with her appearance she went downstairs to lay the breakfast table.

The dogs had settled down and were snoozing in their basket, but Nip opened an eye and Tuck cocked an ear as she opened the bread bin.

"Not for you, girls," she said with a laugh and carried on with her preparations, laying the scrubbed beech table with a jug of milk, glasses of fruit juice, a jar of home-made marmalade and the hand-thrown earthenware side plates with their matching cereal bowls that she had found the previous summer on one of her many painting excursions.

The potter who had made them had set up his studio in a disused watermill nearby and as an artist herself, Isobel felt it was important to support him and indeed any other local craftsmen or women wherever possible. She thought also, that too many people went for convenience over quirky and original. It was much too easy to visit the local supermarket or department store to buy whatever was on the shelves there without so much as a thought for the small local designer or artisan who might find it impossible to compete with the mega manufacturers who, in any case, were limited by price and quality control. Each piece the potter produced was by its very nature unique, which suited Isobel perfectly and held an irresistible charm for her.

Adrian appeared at the kitchen door in due course, washed, dressed and with his hair and beard neatly combed, having collected the local newspaper from the front doormat on his way through to the kitchen.

"Any chance of some bacon this morning?" he asked plaintively.

"No chance at all," she replied firmly. "I have a casserole to prepare for lunch and the dogs to take for a walk before our visitors arrive, so it's muesli and toast for you."

"Can I do anything to help?" Adrian asked, already knowing the answer. His wife was nothing if not capable, despite her artistic leanings and he had learned over the years that she was better left to get on with things on her own when she had a lot to do. Apart from which, she always claimed that he had two left hands and he only got in the way. This arrangement suited him very well and he had no plans to change it; it was her independent spirit that had attracted him to her in the first place and he loved her for it.

"No, thanks, darling. You could walk down to the farm shop for some milk though, if you like. There's only just enough left in the jug for breakfast."

Adrian nodded and sat down at the table. Nip and Tuck ignored him, but their hungry eyes followed Isobel, who was heading for the table with a rack full of toast. She glanced towards the dogs saying encouragingly, "Good girls, stay there," as she delivered the toast to the breakfast table without mishap.

"What's the weather like?" asked Adrian, noticing that they still needed the light switched on. "Have you been outside this morning?"

"A bit misty, but I think it might lift later," she said, looking at her husband and thinking how attractive he still was to her; especially with his beard neatly trimmed and wearing the thick cream shirt and blue cord slacks she had bought him for Christmas.

He had never been her idea of a typical bank manager, even when he had been *her* bank manager and for her it had been love at first sight. It had taken a little longer to persuade him that they had a future together, she thought fondly and there had been many twists and turns in their relationship before she had finally encouraged him to visit one of her art exhibitions and he had realised over dinner later, that he was attracted to her too, but she was nothing if not single-minded, rather like her daughter and once she had made up her mind, that was it.

Fortunately their move to the Lake District had been a joint decision and she had not needed her powers of persuasion to get him there, even though it was a far cry from London where they had first met and light years away from the world of banking. The call of the hills had been too strong to resist and their mutual love of the outdoors had brought them fortuitously to Hardale and 'The Old Schoolhouse'.

The old stone building was set apart from the others in the village and dated back to Victorian times. It had actually been the village school that Isobel had attended as a child, but after a new state-of-the-art school had been built just a few miles away, all the children had been transferred and the empty building had been snapped up by an enterprising young architect. He had, in due course, converted it into a comfortable family house with three bedrooms which he had lived in himself for a while before selling it on to Isobel and Adrian in the 1980s as their holiday home.

It had been much like any other school building of that era with its two chimneys and bell standing proud of its slate roof and high-set casements but it now sported modern double-glazed windows set off by a substantial solid oak front door which was liberally peppered with small, black-headed nails and dominated by an impressive black iron knocker in the shape of a lion's head that was set squarely in the middle.

Although the chimneys were still there, the bell had long gone and the playground had been transformed into a sweeping gravel driveway at the front of the house and an attractive garden at the back. The Flynns had made a few alterations themselves to accommodate a studio in which Isobel could carry on painting while they were staying there and they had also worked hard on the garden which had only boasted two rhododendron bushes, an apple tree and some straggly grass when they had first taken possession.

The apple tree and rhododendron bushes were still there, but the straggly grass had made way for a lush green lawn and Isobel had planted as many bulbs as she could fit into the borders amongst her hardy shrubs so that in the spring the garden was a riot of colour. The vegetable patch was Adrian's pride and joy and he lovingly tended the carrots, beans and potatoes that did surprisingly well year on year.

As he got up from the table having finished eating his meagre breakfast and looking through the local paper which was delivered without fail each Saturday whatever the weather, by a very hardy and tenacious paperboy, he looked down at his wife who was finishing off her glass of orange juice. The dogs looked up at him hopefully, but they were out of luck on this occasion; dogs were not on Adrian's agenda and he did not notice their eager faces nor their wagging tails. Nip and Tuck both put their noses on their paws and looked dejectedly up at Isobel instead, hoping for more success with her.

"I'll wind the clocks first and then walk down to fetch the milk," he said and then turning to go, he added as an afterthought, "Who is collecting your mother?"

"Dash it, I had forgotten Mum," said Isobel, annoyed with herself for not factoring this vital task into her busy schedule. "Could you go and fetch her darling? I don't think I will have time."

"I'm glad I'm still useful for something," he said with a smile. "Of course I will. What time will our visitors be arriving?"

"Probably about eleven-ish," she replied, putting the glass down beside her plate and getting up out of her chair.

The Grandfather clock in the hall struck ten, swiftly followed by ten melodious chimes from the mantel clock in the lounge.

"I had better hurry up and get that casserole in the oven," said Isobel, with which comment she too left the table, taking with her some of the dirty dishes and a retinue of two very eager and excited dogs. But Nip and Tuck were out of luck, yet again.

"Not yet, you two, you will have to wait for your walk. *Down,*" she said firmly.

2

Pippa was feeling at one with the world. She could not quite believe that she was actually in the Lake District standing beside a lake with the man of her dreams by her side. He had chosen their hotel well, she thought, albeit more by good luck than good management, but it was no less perfect for that.

The hotel had the feel of a rambling country house about it, with its log fire smouldering in the wide brick hearth of the spacious low-ceilinged lounge and the well-trodden parquet floor that was scattered at random with faded fringed rugs that had seen better days. She had cast her professional eye over the many and varied china ornaments that she had noticed tastefully displayed to best advantage on window sills and occasional tables in a rather haphazard fashion and, in her opinion, they would have done very well in the auction rooms. Likewise the rather nice old oil paintings of eager-looking terriers that graced the walls of the entrance hall and the one of a stag at bay in its heavy and ornate plaster-moulded frame that stared rather mournfully down on the world at large from its position over the bar.

All around the downstairs rooms were comfy armchairs placed strategically in secluded corners and there was a well-upholstered wing chair to one side of the fireplace that Ian had already tried out for size. Their room had dramatic gold brocade drapes at the windows, crisp white sheets on the king-size bed and gilt regency-style furniture to finish it off.

Pippa had also been pleasantly surprised at the food served for dinner by candlelight the night before as it had been delicious, very well presented and impeccably served by an affable host and his efficient wife. As she watched Ian taking in the view, she smiled to herself with pleasure and waited quietly for his verdict.

Ian breathed in the cold February air and thought that the website had been very accurate in its description of the majestic fells. It was a dull morning and the tops of the fells were hidden from view by very low, grey cloud but the dramatic impact was none the less very obvious. The lake itself was like a huge expanse of opaque glass, barely moving apart from the gentle lapping of the waves on the gravel shore when a duck landed or took off again. Of the snowdrops Pippa had admired so much at Le Vignot, there was no sign, but there were clumps of daffodils in bud all around the lake under the trees, still empty of leaves so early in the year.

He gazed about him in silence, taking it all in. He could well understand her affinity with the mountains and lakes; he felt it himself. Finally, he was ready to share his thoughts with Pippa.

"This place is really rather special," he said slowly and with feeling. "It makes you aware of how insignificant human beings really are."

"That's very profound, Ian," said Pippa, impressed. She was a bit taken aback at the depth of his feelings and was reminded of something she had once read somewhere, 'the more you see of someone, the more of someone you see'. It made her realise that there was still much about Ian that she did not know and it seemed to her that watching his character unfold was like dipping into the pages of a good book. Admittedly, she had only skimmed through the first few chapters so far, but she liked what she had read and was keen to get back to the story and figure out the rest of the plot, so she continued eagerly, "I have never seen it that way myself, but now I think about it, I know exactly what you mean. There's plenty more for you to see. I'd like to show you a waterfall in full flow and actually climb up one of the fells with you perhaps, if there's time."

"Well I suppose we might get through some of that," he said smiling at her eagerness to introduce him to the 'full experience'. "My first challenge though, is to meet your parents. What are they like?" Ian asked and he pulled her arm through his as they strolled back towards the hotel.

"Let's see now," she started. "Mum is very chatty and Dad is not. *I* think they are quite nice, but I'm biased of course," she said with a giggle and then she added just to tease him, "I think that as long as you like dogs, you'll be fine."

"Actually, I've always wanted a dog of my own," was Ian's wistful reply.

"I hope Nip and Tuck don't put you off then," she said. "They *are* extremely lively but they're also very affectionate and intelligent too and for all their bounciness they do look quite sweet when they eventually curl up together in their basket," said Pippa, obviously very fond of the dogs in question.

"Did you say your Dad was a bank manager before he retired?" asked Ian, returning to his main line of questioning.

"Yes he was. He moved all over the place with his job but finally ended up in Linchester when I was about five," said Pippa. "Actually he took early retirement because he said he didn't like the smaller banks being swallowed up by international giants who eventually took the personal touch out of banking. Dad liked to be on first-name terms with most of his customers and found it very satisfying to help them out if there was some financial problem or other, without having to jump through hoops first. They must have moved up here permanently, about seven years ago, I think," she said, realising as she said it that with all their chatting they had arrived back at the hotel again. "Before we go and see Mum and Dad though, there's somewhere else I want to take you," she said mysteriously then added with a grin, "But we'll need the car to get there."

"What am I in for now?" asked Ian in mock trepidation, but Pippa would only make one more comment, "A bit of culture! Come on."

Ian wondered, as Pippa directed him down yet another winding lane with steep banks either side and overhanging trees, where on earth she was taking him. He had no idea that Isobel Flynn was a well-known artist in Cumbria. Not only was she renowned for her watercolours of local beauty spots, but she had quite a following for her abstract and more conventional oil paintings too. Currently she had an exhibition of her paintings on view in a hall some ten miles away from Hardale and this was Pippa's intended destination. She had remembered that Ian wanted to buy some modern art for his newly decorated sitting room and thought the exhibition might help him to crystallise his ideas.

As they drove into a little village with two identical rows of picturesque stone cottages set neatly behind their dry stone walls, leading up to an equally picturesque stone church with a glistening slate spire and they drove over a rustic bridge spanning a fast flowing stream, which would not have looked out of place as the subject for any self-respecting jigsaw puzzle, Pippa finally said, "Here we are Ian. You can stop now, just park in the road over there, by that sweet shop."

Ian obediently stopped the car where Pippa had indicated and his eye was immediately drawn to a large and colourful poster displayed on a sandwich board across the road. It was placed strategically on the pavement outside what looked very much like an old-fashioned village hall. The poster, which was cleverly designed and printed on a red background with black and white lettering, declared with panache:

ARTS AND CRAFTS EXHIBITION
Including paintings by local artist
ISOBEL FLYNN

Ian turned to look at Pippa, who was trying very hard to say nothing and declared in some surprise, "You never told me your mother was an artist! Are you keeping secrets from me already?"

"Not at all," she said with a giggle. "Life would be very dull if there weren't a touch of the unexpected now and then. Anyway, I thought that if you had a look round this exhibition, it might help you to decide what you would like to see hanging in your sitting room. After all, you admired the pictures in my flat and Mum painted all of those," explained Pippa in her own defence.

"OK, I'll let you off this time," he said, quite pleased that she had remembered his throwaway comments of a couple of weeks ago. "Let's get in there."

Inside, through some double doors, the hall had highly-polished wooden floorboards and small-paned windows set high up on the white painted walls through which the light came streaming in. Although it was still early, the exhibition already had several visitors who were wandering about the hall, stopping now and then when a particular exhibit caught their eye and Isobel's works of art were sharing the space with displays of pottery, a stand full of walking sticks with their handles carved into the shapes of animals' heads and some very attractive and unusual jewellery, all crafted by local people. Ian and Pippa picked up a catalogue of the paintings from a pile neatly stacked up on a side table and started their viewing.

There were screens standing side by side down the middle of the hall upon which Isobel's paintings were displayed, alongside all manner of paintings and framed photographs by other contributors. She had put three or four of her oil paintings of abstract art into the exhibition, as well as about twenty of her popular watercolours of local scenes and two small portraits of Nip and Tuck, one of them with the puppies curled up in their basket. Ian noticed that some of the paintings sported little red stickers in one corner which on reading the catalogue more carefully he discovered, meant that they had been bought but not collected as yet. He and Pippa wandered around discussing the pros and cons of the various pictures but Ian found it impossible to make up his mind although he liked the style of Isobel's work very much.

"I thought I wanted something a bit abstract," he said with a worried expression on his face. "But now I've had a look at all the others, I think what I would actually like is one of the watercolours instead. I like your Mum's use of pastel shades and the way all these pictures look so sunny and peaceful, but as I'm not familiar with any of the places she's painted, I don't know which one to pick," was his final conclusion.

"Well, you don't have to buy any at all," said Pippa stating the obvious. "I just thought that seeing so many pictures all together would give you a chance to see what really appealed to you and if the exhibition has made you think a bit more, that's good."

She couldn't help noticing that the young couple in front of her had just bought one of Isobel's watercolours of Ashness Bridge and they were waiting for it to be thoroughly cocooned in bubble wrap before they placed it with immense care into a large and rather muddy rucksack. Ian had also noticed what the young couple had chosen to buy and when Pippa turned round to see if he was watching what was going on, he winked at her knowingly, which gave her a warm glow. It made her feel a sense of togetherness with Ian and tremendous pride in her mother's artistic ability.

"I've just got to have that dear little picture of Nip and Tuck in their basket," she cooed, showing Ian exactly which picture she meant. "Look, don't you think they're cute?" she asked him. Ian nodded at her in affectionate amusement and while Pippa made her way over to the reception desk to make her purchase, Ian had one last look around.

3

As Ian drove up the hill towards The Old Schoolhouse some time later, he was very impressed by its charm and said as much to Pippa.

"You can see why I love it," she said. "And when the clouds lift, you will be able to see right across to Helm Crag which is an impressive sight."

"I quite understand why they chose this particular spot," said Ian. "Although," he added as an afterthought, "I expect it can get quite cut off up here in the middle of winter."

"Don't forget my mother grew up round here and both my parents have lived up here long enough to have experienced most of the harsh conditions. They have a big freezer, an open fire, a log store and a good supply of candles, plus their Land Rover," said Pippa very matter of factly, ticking off all the contingency measures on her fingers and then adding cheerfully for good measure, "So that means they can eat, keep warm and get from A to B if the weather is really bad and Dad also has a little generator tucked away in the garage in case the electricity is cut off for any length of time. I've spent quite a few Christmases up here actually and it's rather nice to be marooned then, but of course I haven't had to get to work. If I had, it really would have been a bit of a bind I admit. Well, this is it Ian, 'The Old Schoolhouse'. What do you think?" she asked as they pulled into the broad gravel driveway through two very heavy wooden gates which someone had thoughtfully left open for them.

"Very impressive," said Ian and meant it.

He parked his car on the drive of The Old Schoolhouse beside a covered log store and noticed to his surprise that there was an old cream Morris Traveller standing under a tarpaulin near the side gate.

"I haven't seen one of those cars around for years. My Dad had one like that when Mike and I were children," he said to Pippa as they got out of the car.

"How funny. Yet another example of our parallel lives," said Pippa with a smile. "That one is my mum's car, 'Daisy'."

"Oh, is it? As our car got older," Ian carried on, warming to his theme, "It had a nasty habit of breaking down just as we were ready to go somewhere important, much to my mother's annoyance, so quite often on a Sunday afternoon Dad would be tinkering with the engine and I was allowed to help him. It was great fun, but rather a messy job I seem to remember. That one must be over forty years old," he finished admiringly.

At that moment the front door opened and Isobel came outside to greet them. As she hugged Pippa, Ian was amazed at how alike they were, both with the same expressive green eyes and distinctive auburn hair. Pippa, released from her mother's grasp, turned to Ian and said, "Ian this is my mother, Isobel." Ian smiled broadly at Isobel and went to shake her hand, but Isobel deliberately ignored his outstretched hand and hugged him warmly as well.

"You are very welcome Ian, come inside both of you and tell me all your news," she said, leading the way into the house.

Ian and Pippa followed Isobel through the massive front door and Ian couldn't help but notice the three heavy black wrought iron hinges on which it was hung and then he stopped for a minute or two to admire the magnificent knocker. He closed the door behind him with a satisfying thud and found himself in a small porch with a glazed inner door leading straight on to the hall, which in turn opened out through two panelled doors into an L shaped sitting room with a vaulted ceiling, which Ian reckoned must once have been the old school hall.

The first thing he noticed after that was the ticking of clocks and the whining of dogs shut away somewhere. He could smell the faint aroma of coffee and also delicious wafts of Isobel's chicken casserole which was cooking slowly in the oven.

Isobel was not a bit like his own mother had been because for a start, she was probably a good fifteen years younger than Vera Chisholm and very Bohemian in her dress, whereas his mother had favoured a more conservative style.

Over the course of the next few minutes the dogs' whining turned to barking, which in turn reached a crescendo so that it was completely impossible for any conversation to be heard until Isobel went to let them in.

Two brown and grey woolly tornadoes, seemingly all legs, tails and wet noses, greeted Pippa enthusiastically and then they both gave Ian the once over after which they finally decided that everything was in order and they settled down in the sitting room, beside Isobel's feet.

"Oh well, you've *obviously* got their seal of approval, Ian," said Isobel with a friendly smile. Ian smiled back and said he was pleased to hear it.

"They have *obviously* got very good taste," said Pippa and she smiled too. "We went to view your exhibition this morning Mum and I just had to have one of your little oils of the dogs," she added, then noticing that her father was nowhere to be seen she asked, "Where's Dad?"

"He has gone to fetch your gran, he won't be long. Would you like some coffee? What did you think of my latest efforts? You didn't have to buy one you know Pippa, I would have done one especially for you. How was the journey?"

"Yes please, very impressed and uneventful, in that order," said Pippa with a laugh. Isobel got up to fetch the coffee while Pippa followed her out of the room to see if she could help and Ian, now left alone in the room with the dogs who were dozing in front of the fire, had time to look around.

The sitting room boasted a large open fireplace crafted out of Lakeland stone and a magnificent polished blue slate hearth. A fire was burning merrily in the grate, spitting from time to time as the damp logs dried out. The walls were painted in a pale shade of apricot, which gave the impression of sunlight in the room on even the greyest of days and an expensive cream carpet covered the floor. There was a small oak writing desk standing underneath one of the windows and two large armchairs plus a three-seater settee placed in front of the fire, each one with soft well-filled cushions and draped in loose cotton covers imprinted with a bright floral design.

There were paintings hanging on the walls and thick, cream, lined curtains at the windows, all of which gave Ian the impression of a very comfortable and welcoming room.

He could see the well-maintained back garden out of the double-glazed French windows and noticed that it was completely enclosed by a stout wooden fence, which he thought was just as well with two terriers likely to try and get out, not to mention the sheep wandering on the fells who might try to get in.

He counted three clocks in that room alone and he found their gentle ticking quite mesmeric and relaxing, so much so that he felt his head nodding but a few moments later he heard voices just outside the door as Isobel and Pippa returned with the coffee and he opened his eyes with a start.

"Pippa says you have milk but no sugar, I hope that's right," said Isobel, handing him a blue and white striped mug. Ian opened his mouth to tell her that it was exactly how he liked his coffee, when a car horn sounded outside and they all heard the Land Rover crunching the gravel and drawing up in the drive.

"Here they are at last," said Isobel and she waltzed off to the front door, her ankle-length multi-coloured skirt spinning behind her and her long string of oversized amber beads clicking together like so many dice in a pot.

"What do you think?" whispered Pippa to Ian as she sat herself beside him on the settee.

"Your Mum is lovely and so like you, it's uncanny," Ian whispered back. "I love this house, too. What's the story with all the clocks?"

"That's Dad. He inherited one from an old aunt and has been buying some more every so often when the fancy takes him. I don't think he will be happy until there is one in every room. It wouldn't surprise me if he ticks himself to sleep at night," replied Adrian's irreverent daughter confidentially, with a cheeky grin.

Ian stood up as a tall, rangy man with a grey beard and glasses entered the room, supporting a tiny bird-like lady with white hair and two very beady brown eyes glinting behind her steel-rimmed spectacles, whom he settled down into a chair.

"Gran, how are you? Hello Dad, this is Ian," declared Pippa proudly.

Her father walked across and gave her a kiss.

"You look well, Pippa," he said, and then turning away from his daughter and towards Ian, Adrian shook him warmly by the hand and added, "How do you do, Ian."

"How do you do, Mr Flynn," replied Ian politely.

"Adrian, please, no formalities here," said Adrian kindly.

Pippa gave her gran a hug, which was warmly reciprocated, then Edith Gill took Ian's outstretched hand and looking him up and down she said in a gentle and melodic voice with a definite Cumbrian lilt, "This is a handsome one, Pippa. How are you both? I have to say that it is a relief to be sitting down somewhere safe at last. A drive with your father always makes my legs wobble a bit."

Ian listened to the conversation being batted back and forth, and then Pippa's father addressed him directly.

"So what do you think of Cumbria, Ian? Pippa tells me you have never been up here before."

"No, and I can see what I've been missing. I'm hoping the cloud will lift soon so that I can see the fells properly. "

"I expect, after midday, we'll get a better view. We've had quite a lot of rain recently, the end result of which is of course too much moisture in the atmosphere, hence all the low cloud and mist."

"Right," said Ian, wondering what to say next. "I was admiring your clocks before you arrived. Pippa says you have collected quite a few," he said, quite pleased with himself for thinking up a relevant topic for discussion.

"Yes, in fact I bought the one on the fireplace at one of Pippa's auctions," replied Adrian taking the bait and looking at the mahogany-cased English Regency bracket clock ticking away peacefully on the mantelpiece. "It's one of my favourite pieces actually. I was drawn to the pyramid shaped finial and all the brass ornaments on it. I understand you had some success at auction recently."

"I did. I sold one of my mother's old jugs for a lot of money. It was a big surprise for my brother and me. We had no idea that she had owned anything so valuable," replied Ian, then he tried to think of something else to say to keep the conversation going and he suddenly remembered Daisy.

"I noticed a Morris Traveller outside," he began, hopefully. Discussing cars was always a good standby he thought.

"That's my wife's car. Actually it's not going at present, it keeps cutting out and I don't understand why. I think it's a bit temperamental like its owner," said Adrian, a twinkle in his eye knowing his wife was listening, but before she could respond Pippa interjected eagerly, "Ian's father had an old Morris years ago, didn't he Ian?"

"Yes, he did. I think he used to have the same sort of trouble too. Would you like me to have a look at it?"

"Well, if you are sure you don't mind. It is rather cold out there this morning," said Adrian doubtfully.

"I would really like to. I'm not promising that I'll be able to do any good, mind you," said Ian as he and Adrian fetched their coats and went outside leaving Pippa, Isobel and Edith to have a good chat without them.

Adrian fetched a toolbox from the shed and between them, they removed the tarpaulin and lifted the bonnet. Ian then bent over to examine the old engine.

"Mm. It looks quite clean, I can't see any obvious problem but it could be to do with the electrics or the fuel line," he said confidently if a bit inaudibly, his head in the darkest recesses of the engine. After a bit of fiddling and several false starts, he finally had the engine running again and Adrian, very impressed, went back inside to report on their success to his wife, calling for Ian to follow him.

"Isobel, Ian has fixed your car. What do you think of that?"

"It wasn't much really," said Ian modestly, trying to wipe his oily hands on some pieces of kitchen paper that Pippa had thoughtfully passed to him as he came in through the door. "The low tension lead to the coil was loose and I have tightened it up for you."

Ian looked at Pippa, who was smiling encouragingly at him.

"Well done Ian," said Isobel, clearly delighted. "I hate it when I have to borrow the other car. It keeps doing that, but if you could show me where this lead is I might have a go myself, if it happens again. We've just got time before the lunch is ready," she said and bustled Ian outside for him to give her a quick lesson in car maintenance.

Edith looked hard at Pippa and said slowly, "After lunch, I had better read your tealeaves my girl. See what the future has in store for you."

"As if I believe all that stuff, Gran," said Pippa feeling mildly amused.

"The tealeaves never lie, Pippa. We'll see," said her grandmother cryptically.

Lunch was a cheerful meal with much animated chatter and when they had all finished Isobel's casserole followed by a generous portion of homemade cheesecake each, Edith asked for a pot of tea and two cups. Pippa grinned.

"Now we're in for it Ian. Gran is going to read our tealeaves."

"Really, Edith, do you have to?" asked Adrian resignedly.

"You don't mind, do you Pippa?" asked Isobel, pouring out two cups.

"Not at all. I don't believe it anyway," she said sensibly.

"Now then, Ian first. Drink this down and we will see what we can see," said Edith mysteriously, handing Ian a cup and saucer.

"You will have to forgive her," said Isobel dryly. "She is the third child of a third child and thinks she has special powers."

Ian smiled politely and drank his tea, then he handed the almost empty cup back to Edith, who swirled it round three times, turned it upside down to drain a little and then looking inside the cup, she studied the contents very carefully.

"Mm. This is interesting. I see success in a new venture," she declared firmly, "And money coming your way, but there is something else. Do you ever go sailing Ian?"

"I did as a boy, but not any more," he said, wondering what to make of this performance.

"I can't explain it then, there is something in the tealeaves to do with boats or masts, but it's not very clear."

"I see," said Ian quietly, wondering if he could keep his face straight much longer. "Thank you anyway."

"Now it's your turn young lady." Pippa giggled and handed her cup over and after the same swirling routine, Edith concentrated on the higgledy-piggledy tealeaves.

"My, my," she said eventually. "What do we have here? I can see a new branch on your tree of life and a lot of happiness coming your way."

"I *am* glad it's nothing bad," remarked Pippa feeling her mouth twitching, "I'm not going sailing too, am I?"

"Scoff all you like," said Edith with mock indignation. "Just wait and see if I'm right or not."

"We can never tell, Mum," said Isobel wearily. "You don't go into enough detail."

"You have to have faith," said Edith, by now weary of the tealeaves herself. "Using up all that psychic energy has tired me out, so I would like to go home. Who is going to give me a lift?"

"We will," said Pippa straight away. "Ian and I want to go and visit the waterfall before it gets too dark."

"You mean Mill Force?" she asked and Pippa nodded. "That is the nearest. You will both be careful though, won't you? It might be quite treacherous down there after all the rain we've had recently."

"We won't do anything silly," said Pippa reassuringly and Ian also promised not to take any chances so having had her worries put to rest, Edith asked for her coat and Isobel went off to fetch it.

"Do you fancy a walk tomorrow morning if it is fine?" asked Adrian. "There is a circuit round by the beck which should be manageable in a couple of hours.

You know we have plenty of boots you can both borrow if necessary."

"Would you like that, Ian?" asked Pippa. "I'm up for it Dad, especially as we'll be sitting in the car for ages later on tomorrow."

"That sounds good to me, I would like to see a bit more of the countryside," answered Ian. "Perhaps it won't be quite so misty tomorrow." Adrian was able to reassure him on that score, as he listened to the weather forecast on the radio on a daily basis. He understood very well that it was foolish to take chances with the weather on the fells when it could change so quickly and be very different from one hour to the next, never mind day-to-day and he gave them his latest bulletin.

"I checked this morning and apparently tomorrow is due to be much brighter. We are forecast a bit of wind and clear skies," he said as they all walked towards the front door, Edith now snugly wrapped up in her weatherproof quilted coat.

Ian and Pippa made their farewells and after thanking Isobel for a delicious meal, they left with Edith leaning on Ian's arm. Her cottage wasn't far from the hotel, as Pippa had explained to Ian when the trip had first been planned and having safely deposited her at her front door, they made their way over to Mill Force before the daylight had worn itself out.

4

They could hear the water pounding down the craggy fell-side before they could see it and after a steep climb down a slippery bank criss-crossed with treacherously tangled tree roots, the force came into view. Due to the recent days of heavy rainfall, it was a splendid sight with water tumbling and bubbling thunderously down from the mossy top of the fell and cascading in a deafening torrent into the foaming river below. The site took Ian's breath away.

"That is awesome," he yelled, marvelling at the sight before him and Pippa, cupping her hands to her mouth, shouted back at him,

"Quite a sight, isn't it?"

They stayed transfixed for quite a few minutes until they realised how incredibly cold it was so close to all that nearly freezing water and it did not take them long to decide that sitting in the warm lounge at the hotel held much more allure than shivering in the chilly spray of the thundering waterfall.

It was just as Ian was about to step onto the footpath at the top of the bank, behind Pippa, that he heard it. What he had heard, he wasn't quite sure, but he was very sure he had heard something.

"Pippa," he called urgently, "I think there's something down here."

She turned round and peered into the gloom of the path they had just left.

"I can't see anything. Have you got a torch in the car?" she asked quickly.

"Yes, in the boot," he replied and he took the car keys out of his coat pocket and threw them to her. She caught them deftly and disappeared off into the dusk, while Ian waited for her to return, his ears alert for the sound to come again. Pippa was back in a few minutes, this time carrying the torch, which she switched on and had a brief look about. There was nothing.

"It was down that way," said Ian, pointing towards a dead tree at the left of the path. Pippa directed the beam of light over to the tree, but they could still see nothing. It was getting darker by the minute and just as Pippa made one last sweep with the torch, they both heard the noise.

"I'm coming down," said Pippa with purpose.

"Be careful," urged Ian. "We don't know what it is yet."

As they both scrambled over the mass of tree roots and thick carpet of brown, rain-soaked leaves in the general direction of the dead tree they heard the noise for a third time. It was louder than before and shortly afterwards, in the beam of the torch, they saw two luminous and very scared eyes.

It was a small dark brown dog, ears flattened, eyes staring, coat covered in mud, cowering in the roots of the dead tree and yelping from time to time.

"Oh, poor thing, can you reach it, Ian?" asked Pippa, distressed.

"Stay there," said Ian, taking charge, "I'll get it out."

The little dog was wet and miserable and looked a pathetic sight. As he reached out to grab it, the dog whimpered again, but Ian had it safely tucked away in his coat without too much trouble and they made their ascent yet again.

Making their way back up was not as easy as getting down had been as it was very nearly pitch black now and Pippa needed her hands to scramble up the bank so she could not hold the torch up to give them a bit of light and help them find the best route. Eventually, after much slipping and sliding, they managed to reach the top and then they hurried along the footpath and back to the warmth and safety of the car.

"Brr. My fingers are freezing," shivered Pippa, rubbing her hands together.

"I'll put the heater on, you'll soon warm up when we get going," said Ian turning the engine on and the heater up full blast as he spoke. "Now, what are we going to do about this little bag of bones?" he asked, examining the dog in the car-light.

"It must have been down there a while, it's so thin and bedraggled," said Pippa.

"Not so much of the 'it'. I think she is expecting puppies," said Ian in a surprised tone. As he moved the dog to get a better look, she yelped, two brown eyes watching him steadfastly. "I think she has injured her leg," he finished with some concern.

"I know, we'll take her to the Killingbeck Ridge," said Pippa, coming up with a good idea as usual. "Someone there is bound to know if a dog has gone missing round here. Finding a vet at this time of day and on a Saturday is a non-starter for us." Ian agreed that this was the best plan and they set off for the hotel, Pippa nursing the little dog on her knee, wrapped up in the rug Ian always kept in the car in case he was stranded somewhere and had to spend all night out in the wilds.

"I have always thought of waterfalls as rather romantic, especially the ones you can walk behind," said Pippa, beginning to feel her fingers come back to life. "Rescuing dogs and visiting parents don't come very high up on the romantic scale, though, do they?" she finished ruefully.

"I wouldn't have missed any of it," said Ian loyally. "I enjoyed meeting your parents and of course, your gran. I wonder if her predictions will come true? Perhaps she meant Mike's job offer." Pippa grinned at that. She was glad her grandmother's clairvoyant skills had not fazed Ian but she was very sceptical about them. "As for the dog," he went on, "Well, we couldn't have left her out there injured, now could we?"

"No of course not. You were very brave, Ian, and that *is* romantic. You were even more of a hero for swallowing all gran's mumbo-jumbo but I never take much notice of what she predicts anyhow, so I wouldn't know what she meant. Perhaps we should buy ourselves a boat," she said with a twinkle in her eye. "Gran didn't see this little waif and stray in the tealeaves though, did she?" she went on, gently stroking the little dog's damp head.

As they walked back into the hotel half an hour later, they went straight over to the receptionist and Pippa explained about their rescue of the little dog down by Mill Force.

"Good gracious! It looks like Will Grace's dog Dollie," she said straight away. "It's his farm you can see from the dining room window. His children have been beside themselves as she is their pet and she went missing over a week ago. She looks to me as if she could do with a good feed. Dollie is due to have her puppies in the next few days or so I think. Thank goodness you found her when you did Miss Flynn. I'll ring Quarry Farm at once and then take her down to the kitchens to find her something to eat. They are going to be so pleased when I tell them she is safe and sound."

Pippa handed over the little bundle, still wrapped in Ian's blanket and then both she and Ian headed for the stairs.

"Miss Flynn," called the receptionist a few moments later, stopping them in their tracks, "I almost forgot to tell you with all this excitement. There's a message for you," and she held out a small post-it note as she was speaking. "You had a telephone call about half an hour ago."

Slightly mystified, Pippa backtracked, thanked her and took the note which she scanned quickly and passed the gist of it on to Ian.

"It's from Gran, she wants us to call in and see her before we leave. I wonder what that's all about."

"She has probably had another psychic revelation," laughed Ian. "We'll find out tomorrow. Let's go and book in for dinner, but first we could both do with a hot drink."

Early the next morning and none the worse for their adventure down at the waterfall, Ian and Pippa booked out of the hotel and set off for The Old Schoolhouse and the walk they had arranged with Adrian the day before.

They arrived to find him kneeling on the kitchen floor sorting through a box of walking boots with the help of Nip and Tuck, who seemed to think that all the laces were in the wrong boots or if not, just needed a quick check to see how strong they were. Eventually, having given his visitors a perfunctory greeting and realising he was getting nowhere fast, an exasperated Adrian called his wife.

"Isobel," he thundered, "If you don't deal with these dogs, I will not be responsible for my actions," he said on the verge of losing his temper, retrieving one of the boots he had intended for Pippa from the vice-like grip of Nip's teeth just as Isobel came in through the kitchen door and to the rescue.

"They are only playing," she said soothingly as she picked up both dogs and sat them on her knees, then she swivelled round in her chair to face Ian and Pippa.

"Hello you two, are you feeling energetic?"

"Definitely," replied Pippa enthusiastically, "And we have to tell you about our adventure last night before we go. When we were down at Mill Force, Ian rescued a little dog."

Isobel was all ears and even Adrian stopped what he was doing to listen.

"Apparently she belongs to someone called Will Grace. We think she must have injured her leg and the poor little thing couldn't get back up the bank," said Pippa. Isobel and Adrian looked at each other.

"We know Will. We get our logs from him. He must have been very pleased to get his dog back, how long had she been missing?" asked Isobel cuddling her dogs even closer.

"About a week I think *and* she is expecting puppies," finished Pippa dramatically.

"If it's the dog I think it is, she is a Border terrier cross called Dollie and they are very hardy little dogs, so I expect she will bounce back," said Isobel, "But I'm not so sure about her puppies," she added doubtfully.

"You are right, Mum, it *was* Dollie," said Pippa quietly.

"It's a good job you went down to see the waterfall when you did then, or it might have been another story entirely for Dollie and her puppies. February is not really the month for sightseeing waterfalls," said Adrian. "Isn't there a local saying 'February fills the dyke', Isobel?" Isobel nodded her head, a concerned expression clouding her brow.

"Yes, all the local people know how hazardous getting down that bank can be in the winter months after a lot of rain and how fast the river runs at that point, so they would keep well away," she informed them very seriously. "Actually you two were very lucky neither of you slipped and twisted an ankle … or worse," she finished, with a little shudder, a certain amount of relief in her voice.

Isobel was not intending to join them on the walk and when she was happy that they were kitted out properly for a ramble on the fells, she left them to it, saying, "I have other things to do."

Adrian understanding her verbal shorthand explained that, loosely translated, it meant she needed to get back to her painting, so without any further delay he ushered Pippa and Ian out into the lane and over a style on the first leg of their ramble round by Kinsey Beck.

5

Edith Gill lived in a small grey stone cottage in the middle of Hardale village. She had been on her own for most of her married life as her husband, Ralph, had been killed in action during the Normandy Landings and she had never married again. They had been promised to each other from the age of twelve and Edith, having been left with Isobel to look after, had never needed anyone else.

Their wedding had been in the village church in May 1939, exactly thirty years before Isobel and Adrian's marriage in the very same church. They had travelled to Blackpool for their honeymoon, but she had never ventured any further south until Isobel had gone to art school in London, and then needed help when her babies had been born.

Edith was happy in her little house with all her memories and she could not understand other people's fascination for visiting foreign parts on a regular basis. After Ralph had been killed, she had wrapped his love around her and got on with looking after their baby girl, with the help of her parents and two sisters. Edith had managed quite well on her allowance from the Army and other benefits, augmented by her cake-making skills. The shop in the village had needed a never-ending supply of her scones, flapjacks and Victoria sponges throughout the summer when the visitors descended in earnest on Hardale and the winter months were taken up with knitting jumpers for Isobel and making all her other clothes from paper patterns designed by Edith herself. Isobel had inherited her artistic genes from her mother and had passed them on in turn to both of her children, which gave Edith tremendous satisfaction.

She was very fond of both her grandchildren, particularly Tim as he reminded her so much of Ralph, but Pippa was the spit of Isobel at the same age, which she found quite disconcerting at times and she had been known to call Pippa, Isobel and vice versa.

Now she had met Ian, Edith felt sure he was the one for Pippa and she had decided to herself that a wedding would soon be on the cards. They suited each other very well she thought and she liked Ian's kind eyes and his quiet ways. Yes, he would do very well for her granddaughter.

Edith wanted to give Pippa a special gift, now her sixth sense told her she would soon be a bride and she had something special in mind. One of her maiden aunts had left her a delicate gold necklace with a diamond drop pendant and noticing Pippa's diamond earrings the day before, she thought they would look very nice together. Especially when worn with a long white dress complete with train and a veil, but now she was getting ahead of herself. Anyway she had no need of such a charming thing. It would show to better advantage on a young neck with a pretty face above it she thought, rather than to draw attention to one well past its sell-by date.

There was something else she wanted to discuss with Pippa too, hence the telephone message. Edith hoped they would not call while she was still at church, but just in case they did, she fixed a note securely to her door before she left to tell them where she was, then she took her stick and set off to walk the few hundred yards or so to the church.

Meanwhile, nearby, Ian and Pippa were just on the way back from their walk with Adrian. He knew the local fells like the back of his hand and he had taken them on a very pleasant meander round past Kinsey Beck as promised. The weather forecast had been fairly accurate and the wind had blown most of the low cloud away from the fell tops, revealing a generous sprinkling of snow. The surrounding fields with their solid dry stone wall boundaries were full of ewes about to give birth and some early lambs were already walking about a little unsteadily. A solitary black lamb was trying to suckle its mother, face upturned and little woolly tail quivering in delight.

Ian stopped for a moment to watch. He was thoroughly enjoying himself. The feel of the springy turf beneath his borrowed boots and the mournful bleating of sheep, together with the fresh scent of the pine trees and the impressive scenery all made a heady mix for his senses to absorb. It was all so different from Linchester and, as Pippa had explained at Le Vignot not so long ago, it was the perfect place for recharging batteries. The walk was over all too soon as far as he was concerned and they arrived back at The Old Schoolhouse to find coffee bubbling on the Aga, but no sign of Isobel.

"I expect she is in the 'Pod'," declared Adrian knowingly, and Pippa, being familiar with her father's ironic nickname for her mother's vehicle into the world of art, headed off in the direction of the studio.

"I know she has a commission to be finished by next week and she hates letting people down," explained Adrian to Ian who was having trouble finally extricating himself from his tightly laced boots.

"Mum, we're back," called Pippa.

On hearing friendly voices, Nip and Tuck started to yap hysterically and when Pippa opened the door, they both shot through it like greyhounds out of the slips closely followed by their mistress in her painting smock, a pair of very fetching blue and green framed glasses perched on the end of her nose, who was trying to control their exuberance to very little effect.

"Hello girls, are you pleased to see me?" said Pippa, laughing at their antics and she made a fuss of both of them. The dogs finally quietened down and ran into the kitchen, tails wagging and a look of entreaty in their eyes as they faced Isobel.

"We'll go out for a walk later," she said kindly, removing her spectacles and patting their soft, closely-cropped curly heads gently. "Now settle down you two."

"Do you mind if I ask you something?" asked Ian who had been watching this pantomime with a grin on his face.

"Not at all, what is it Ian?" Isobel asked as she sat down at the kitchen table.

"I was just wondering why your dogs have such unusual names," he said boldly.

"Now you've done it Ian. Isobel and a captive audience are to be avoided at all cost," said Adrian wryly, but Isobel, deliberately ignoring her husband's good-natured jibe, proceeded to give Ian's question the sensible answer it deserved.

"Well, I think women these days face far too much pressure to keep themselves looking young and staying slim Ian," she started, "I think we should all be allowed to be as nature intended and comfortable in our own skins, so my dogs represent my protest against the current trend for cosmetic surgery on everything; reducing this, sucking out that and plumping up the other. As an artist,

I like to paint people as they really are, warts and all," she declared with feeling, a sparkle in her eye. Ian was simultaneously amused and surprised at her candid reply, but made no comment apart from a non-committal, "I see," which was all that was necessary because Adrian added his own acerbic rider.

"There you have it, my wife's bête noir, the Barbie Doll culture! Actually, I must say that I have to agree with every word. Now then, shall I pour out the coffee?"

"We haven't got long, Dad. Gran rang last night and left us a message that she wanted to see us before we left, so just a small cup please."

"What time is it?" asked Isobel, unable to see the kitchen clock from where she was sitting.

"Five to eleven," replied Adrian, handing round the cups.

"Mum will still be in church then, so you have at least half an hour I should think. Do you need some food for the journey? There is a nice piece of quiche in the fridge. Or some fruit?" suggested Isobel.

"What do you think, Ian?" Pippa asked.

"I don't particularly want to eat at the motorway services, so a bite of something would be good. Thanks, Isobel," he replied, thinking how welcome Pippa's family had made him and how genuine and very interesting they all were.

He had so much to tell Mike and Gaynor on his return. He had tried to take some pictures with his phone, but he felt that his brother and his wife would have to see Cumbria for themselves to really appreciate the charm of the place.

On their walk that morning Ian had had time to mull over Mike's job offer once more while Adrian and Pippa had been discussing work and finances together for part of the walk and he had finally made his decision. Had he been in Linchester he would have been at his brother's house for lunch and could have told him exactly what conclusion he had come to there and then but as he was not, Mike would have to wait until Monday morning. Then Pippa's voice entered his subconscious, bringing him back from his thoughts about his brother and Linchester and once more into the warm kitchen of The Old Schoolhouse.

"I wonder how Dollie is today after her ordeal. Do you think we will ever find out?"

"Yes you will," said Isobel, "I'll go and see Will Grace myself and ask him for a progress report," she added helpfully.

"Could you ring me as soon as you know anything?" asked Pippa.

"Of course I will," replied her mother kindly.

"We forgot to tell you about Tim," said Pippa, satisfied with her mother's reply and suddenly remembering her brother's news.

"What is he up to?" asked Adrian. Dogs never rated highly on his Richter scale of interesting topics, but his son did. Unfortunately Tim managed the trip up north less frequently than Pippa did and his parents had to make do with their spasmodic phone calls to him and his even less frequent ones to them.

"It was all Ian's doing," said Pippa proudly. "Without his help Tim would still be messing round now, trying to find someone to listen to his music and set him off into the music world proper, but Ian introduced him to a recording agent and they are in the process of sorting him out."

"Come on Pippa, it was more Garth than me. Tim certainly has talent and it would only have been a matter of time before Nimbus would have taken off, with or without my help."

"I suppose you're right," said Pippa, accepting Ian's rebuke with good grace. "I am very fond of Tim but he has never been very dynamic," commented Tim's affectionate sister.

Her parents on hearing this exchange, were pleased to see that Pippa had at last found a man with a bit of character, who wasn't going to let her be the driving force the whole time. Adrian in particular was pleased to see that his reading of Ian's personality had been correct and he felt very comfortable with the idea of Ian becoming a permanent fixture in his family if that was the way things were headed. Pippa was a very sensible girl and he loved her dearly, but he also recognised the managing streak in her personality which was an undoubted asset in her chosen career but not such a blessing in her relationships with men. Ian was quite clearly able to hold his own with Pippa which, in his opinion, was a very healthy sign.

Isobel, for her part, was now planning her wedding outfit; as far as she was concerned, it was only a matter of time.

6

Edith let herself into the house and took off her hat and coat, hanging them tidily on the hallstand and propping her stick up against the wall. It was lovely, she thought to herself, to be able to come back into a nice warm house. The old church could be relied upon to be deliciously cool in the summer, but equally it was rather cold and draughty in the winter and it was at times like these that she was very glad of her central heating even though she still liked to have an open fire burning in her front room as well.

She walked straight through to her spotless and well-ordered kitchen and switched the kettle on, then she took a Victoria sponge cake out of the round cake tin in her kitchen cupboard. Next came a pretty cut glass plate which she dressed with a paper doily and setting the cake on the top, she stood back to admire her handiwork. As she was deciding whether to offer her visitors teacups or mugs, someone knocked at her front door. Edith, always conscious of wanting to look her best, quickly pulled down the cardigan of her warm pink lambswool twin set so that it rested tidily over the top of her navy blue skirt without a crease in sight and she went off to see who it was.

"Hello Edith, I need a favour," said a short woman in a sensible grey tweed coat, as Edith opened the door. Her visitor's age was uncertain, but she had brown curly hair and a healthy demeanour topped off with a very cheerful smile. Edith knew her well, it was Maddy Smith from church. "I had to come round to your house because you left before I could catch you after the service," she explained pleasantly.

"Hello Maddy," said Edith looking slightly surprised, then it was her turn to explain. "Yes, I had to get back home quickly this morning because I am expecting visitors," she said. "I didn't have time for coffee and a chat this morning."

"I won't keep you long, I just wondered if you could give me your granddaughter's address in Linchester, if you don't mind. She rescued Dollie yesterday and my grandchildren want to write and thank her."

"Well I never!" declared Edith, cups, cake and kettle forgotten. She ushered Maddy into her cosy sitting room where she was regaled with the tale of the little dog's dramatic rescue. Then, after a very brief chat about dogs in general, Edith took a piece of paper from the pad beside her telephone and noted down Pippa's address for her friend as swiftly as she could, because Maddy did not have time to wait for Ian and Pippa to arrive to be thanked in person. Her husband, not famous for his easy-going nature, was waiting outside for her in their car with the engine running and he expected his roast dinner to be on the table at one-thirty sharp.

As soon as Maddy had left the house, Edith got back to the job in hand. She hoped that Pippa and Ian would arrive very soon as she wanted to hear exactly what had happened down at the waterfall from the heroine herself. Having finally decided on cups and saucers, she then went to sit by the fire whilst she waited for them to arrive, softly humming the tune of 'Hills of the North rejoice' to herself interspersed with the odd few words of that hymn that she could remember.

Meanwhile, Ian and Pippa were putting the promised quiche in an unwanted ice cream tub due to the lack of any other suitable receptacle being found and taking their leave of Nip and Tuck, who seemed rather reluctant to let them go. In the end Isobel had to shut the dogs out in the back garden while she and Adrian went to see their daughter on her way.

She gave Ian a quick hug and Pippa an extra long one, just giving her time to whisper in her daughter's ear, "He is perfect, Pippa, make sure you hold on to him and don't leave it so long before your next visit."

"Thanks Mum, I am going to try and now Ian has seen how lovely it is up here, I am sure he will want to come again soon too."

Adrian, for his part, shook Ian's hand.

"It was good to meet you, drive safely now. Next time you come, I will plan a more adventurous route up the fell for you."

"I have enjoyed my visit very much. I'll start training as soon as I get back home," promised Ian with a broad grin.

Adrian patted him on the back kindly and went over to Pippa.

"Goodbye for now sweetie. Don't give Ian too much of a hard time," he said with a smile.

"As if I would," said Pippa and gave her father a kiss on both cheeks before she got into the car beside Ian.

Isobel and Adrian were growing ever smaller in the car's rear view mirror and Pippa sighed.

"I'm always sad when it's time to leave," she said wistfully, "It's not only that I'm going to miss Mum and Dad themselves, but the whole feeling of being in amongst the hills and lakes," she explained.

"Well, I know it's not much consolation, but I feel a bit down myself," said Ian with a rueful smile. "We haven't really had that much time to look around the area with the days being so short, have we? We must definitely come back again soon. You were quite right Pippa, I do like it here," he finished, hoping he had been some sort of comfort to her.

"I was hoping you would feel like that," said Pippa cheering up a bit. "I reckoned that once you had seen Cumbria for yourself, you would appreciate the magic. At least we still have a couple of hours left and our visit to Gran before we have to head for the motorway."

Edith was at her front door as soon as the car drew up outside her house and she welcomed them both warmly.

"A little bird told me that you were very busy yesterday evening after you dropped me off," she said in her attractive Cumbrian lilt as she ushered them into her front room. "Come in and tell me all about it."

"News travels fast round here Gran. Have you had your spies out?" said Pippa innocently with a twinkle in her eye. "Tell us what you've heard and then we can tell you the *true* story."

"My information is that you rescued a dog from the waterfall," replied Edith, expertly dividing the cake into eight equal slices.

"Almost right," said Pippa slowly. "It was Ian who rescued the dog, in fact the whole adventure was down to him. I was half way back up to the car when he heard a noise and when we investigated further it turned out to be a bedraggled little dog with an injured leg. The receptionist at the hotel said she belonged to the people up at Quarry Farm, so we left it to her to let them know. As you have heard all about it, Dollie must have got home safely."

"Yes, she did. Oh, I *see*. I was told it was *you* who rescued the dog Pippa. My informant was Will Grace's mother-in-law and she told me that sadly, Dollie has a broken leg. When they called out the farm vet yesterday evening he could not tell them for certain if all the puppies are still all right. I suppose they won't know for sure until they are born. Anyway, she now has her leg in a plaster and is apparently hopping about on three legs quite cheerfully and seems much better in herself," she said, finally sitting down having passed round the cups of tea and plates of cake while she was talking.

"What a relief. I'm glad I heard her when I did or the whole story might have had a very different ending," said Ian, swallowing a piece of cake. "This cake is really delicious, Edith. What's your secret?"

"Years of practice," laughed Edith. "Now, before I forget, I have something to give you Pippa," she said handing her granddaughter a small black leather box with a tiny gold button on its side. "This belonged to my mother's sister, your great great-aunt Win."

"What is it, Gran?"

"Open it and see," said Edith tantalisingly, so Pippa opened the box and then gasped as she saw the pretty necklace.

"Before you say anything Pippa," said Edith brooking no arguments, "I want you to have it now because I don't wear it any more and I thought it would look lovely with those earrings of yours."

"Oh Gran, how sweet of you, I'll put it on straight away. Thank you so much," said Pippa and she gave her gran a kiss. "Will you do it up for me Ian?" she asked. "Actually Ian gave me the earrings. They were his mother's and they will make a lovely set with your necklace." Ian gallantly obliged, while Edith looked on approvingly.

"Perfect," she declared with pleasure when the catch was finally secure. "Now for the main reason why I left you that message yesterday," said Edith and she reached behind her chair to produce a medium-sized brown cardboard box tied up with string.

"What have you got there?" Pippa asked, intrigued.

"Do you remember Dorrie Swift who owned the cake shop in the village?" she asked and Pippa nodded. "Well, she died last year and left me this. I don't really know what it is supposed to be and I have enough clutter already so I wondered if you could sell it for me at your auction house. Have a look and see what you think."

Pippa untied the string and opened the box, then she separated the bubble wrap to find a large and colourful oriental porcelain bowl decorated inside and out with beautifully painted chrysanthemums in a burnt umber shade. The intricate pattern was not one Pippa recognised.

"This is very nice indeed, Gran," said Pippa admiringly. "It is a Japanese Imari bowl, probably about eighty years old. I can't say exactly how much you might get for it at auction, but I will guess at about five hundred pounds as I don't know the pattern. I can certainly find out though. When I get back home, I'll look it up in my reference book and let you know."

"That's fine lovey, anything it fetches will be a bonus and I would rather that than keep it hidden away in a box under the stairs," said Edith in a down-to-earth fashion. "It *is* a very attractive pattern, now I look at the bowl again and I would like it to go to someone who will really appreciate it," she added, then having dealt with her auction business, Edith turned her attention to other matters. "Now then, Ian, have you enjoyed your stay up here?"

"Very much indeed," he replied straight away. "I was saying to Pippa in the car on the way here that we should come back again soon, when the days are longer and the weather is a bit warmer and when we have a bit more time. I would love to climb one of the fells."

This was music to Edith's ears. Anything that encouraged more frequent visits from Pippa got her vote and she smiled happily.

They carried on talking about what Ian could see on his next visit and before they knew it, it was time for them to leave on the last leg of their journey.

Ian left the house first, collecting a hug from Edith on the way and taking the box with him as he went to open the car.

"Goodbye Pippa and see if you can't add another diamond to your collection by the next time I see you - this time on your finger," said Edith fearlessly. "I know young people these days live together at the drop of a hat, but marriage is much more rewarding and a good basis for a strong relationship, especially when the difficult times come … and they do. Anyone who tells you otherwise lives in cloud cuckoo land. Oh yes and one last thing," she added, "Take this with you, it was your Grandad's," she said as she handed Pippa a battered leather briefcase bulging with papers that had been resting under the hall stand partially hidden by Edith's coat and a fine array of sturdy looking umbrellas.

Seeing Pippa beginning to open it, she said hurriedly, "Don't look inside now lovey, wait until you get home," and she gave Pippa a quick hug whilst gently propelling her towards the front door.

"Are you sure that is all? It's not Christmas you know, Gran," said Pippa in a gently teasing fashion.

"Get on with you, you cheeky madam. I know what month it is, I am not gaga yet," said Edith and she waved to them until they were out of sight. Then, with a little sigh, she walked slowly back inside the house.

7

Mike was sitting alone in his office, checking the figures one more time and mindlessly drumming his fingers on the desk. He was positive it would all work and he was hoping against hope that Ian would agree to join him with this new project. Mike did not like waiting around for other people, he had always been one to get on with things himself. He liked to be in charge and everything he tackled had to be done properly, efficiently, but more importantly to him, without undue delay. Consequently, not knowing his brother's decision and having to wait until he returned from his weekend in the Lake District to find out what it was, made him very uncomfortable.

Gaynor, having been married to Mike for nearly twenty-five years, understood this and had tried to keep him occupied all weekend, but now she had run out of ideas and had retired, exhausted, to run a long hot bath.

So Ian and Pippa's return to Linchester was very much looked forward to by both of them, but for very different reasons.

Gaynor, having had her 'five minutes' peace', came downstairs in her dressing gown, her hair knotted up in a pink towel.

"Mike, are you coming upstairs now? It's past midnight."

"I just want to read this through one more time and then I'll join you, I promise," said Mike looking up briefly from his paperwork.

"Don't be too long then, we both need our beauty sleep," she said, brushing his cheek with her lips before wandering back upstairs again, hoping he had meant what he said.

The persistent ringing of the telephone woke Ian from his slumbers. He kept his eyes shut and reached for the phone, but it stopped ringing just as his hand touched the handset. He finally opened his eyes and it took him a moment to remember exactly where he was.

He was in fact safely back home and in his own bed in Linchester, but feeling that momentary disorientation that comes with having had a few days away from familiar surroundings.

The phone started ringing again and this time, Ian picked it up quickly and answered it with a rather weary, "Hello?" simultaneously wondering who on earth could be ringing him so early in the morning. He should have known; it was Mike.

"Hello Ian. Did you have a good trip? I thought I had the wrong number when I rang before. Didn't you hear the phone?" asked his brother rather impatiently.

"Oh, it was *you* was it," said a bleary-eyed Ian, "I was asleep Mike. The phone woke me up and I just didn't reach it in time. We didn't get back until late last night and yes it was a great trip, thanks. I enjoyed meeting Pippa's family and the hotel was excellent. The countryside up there is breathtaking, you and Gaynor really should make the effort and go and see it for yourselves you know," he finished, now wide awake.

"Good," said his brother briskly, ignoring Ian's final comment. "Did you have time to consider my offer at all?"

"As a matter of fact I did," replied Ian, thinking he would keep Mike in suspense for just a fraction of a second longer.

"Well?" Mike asked, close to exploding and finding it very difficult to contain himself.

"Erm, I have weighed up the pros and cons and I have decided … to take you up on your offer," said Ian after which he heard a sharp intake of breath on the other end of the phone and then a much relieved and very cheerful Mike said, "That's fantastic Ian, I am delighted. I'll speak to the bank later on and then we will talk some more."

"Can I get back to sleep now?" asked Ian with a smile, but he was talking to himself. Mike had already rung off.

Pippa, in the meantime, her batteries well and truly charged, had arrived at work carrying with her Edith's cardboard box protecting the unusual Imari bowl. Her research had told her that she had been right in her identification of the bowl and she was just going to check with James McFarlane as to its possible value.

Beth was in the office when Pippa walked in, her long dark hair neatly tied back in a leopard-skin print scrunchie. She was working at the computer, a large box of paper hankies on the desk beside her.

"Morning Beth, did you have a good weekend?" Pippa greeted her cheerfully. Beth looked up, heavy-eyed.

"Definitely *not* a good morning," she said and sniffed loudly. "The weekend was much the same as usual apart from catching a stinking cold," she added dolefully. "I don't have to ask you about yours though, you look amazing."

"Thanks, I feel pretty good," said Pippa, her eyes shining. "Sorry about your cold. Remind me to tell you about the incident with the dog and the waterfall later, but I have just got to show James this bowl first."

"He's in his office, but he's on the phone at the moment," said Beth sneezing loudly. "No," she went on, looking at the indicator panel on her extension, "He has just finished."

"Right, I'll go straight in then," said Pippa walking off quickly so as to catch James before he became embroiled in another lengthy telephone conversation, while Beth gave her poor sore nose yet another vigorous blow.

She found James sitting in his comfortable old red calf-leather chair behind his leather-topped antique partners' desk checking the appointments in his diary for the week ahead.

"Hello, Pippa," he said with a welcoming smile, then noticing the box he added, "Have you got something interesting to show me?"

Pippa took the bowl out of its box and put it gently on the desk in front of him without saying a word. He looked at it carefully and whistled slowly under his breath.

"Ah, Imari. This is a beauty, Pippa. Where did it come from?"

"All the way from Cumbria, courtesy of my grandmother," said Pippa, then she went on to explain the bowl's provenance to James. "So how much do you think? Five hundred pounds?" she ventured.

"Oh, I think we might do better than that," replied James jovially. "This is a very good example of its type. Let's say a reserve of six hundred and hopefully it might reach a thousand if the right people are here on the day. I have one or two contacts who might be very interested to know this will be on offer next month. I'll make a few calls this afternoon when I am back from my probate meeting. Now I have got something to show *you*," he said getting up from his desk. "Come and have a look at this," said James and beckoned to Pippa to follow him as he walked back into the auction hall which was once more an empty womb waiting for the next embryonic items, extraordinary or mundane, to be implanted.

Pippa followed him, still carrying the box which she put down on a display unit while James took down a shrouded garment that was hanging on the wall. He carefully removed the cover to reveal an exquisite, full length Chinese robe made from delicate aquamarine silk, decorated with yellow butterflies and pink lotus blossom and with a dramatic black edging which finished it off perfectly. Pippa's eyes were like saucers. She thought it was quite beautiful.

"It's breathtaking, James, how old is it?"

"Probably close to seventy years old. It is incredible how the colours have kept their vibrancy and it is a shame we will probably only get a hundred pounds for it. When you think of all the work involved in its making, it should be worth ten times that." Pippa agreed with him and a thought popped into her head and flitted about like one of the little yellow butterflies fluttering from blossom to blossom on the Chinese robe, but before she had time to let it settle, James was speaking again.

"I forgot to ask about your weekend up north," he said. "How did it go?"

"Fine thanks, we got on really well. I enjoyed the break and it was lovely to see my family again," said Pippa.

"Mr McFarlane, there's another call for you," said Beth from the office door in a very croaky voice and politely excusing himself, James hurried off to answer the phone while Pippa followed Beth back into the office.

"You don't sound too good at all," she said.

"I'll be all right, but my throat feels like sandpaper and I have a herd of stampeding wildebeest tap dancing in my head," said Beth pathetically, finishing her sentence with yet another sneeze.

"Look," said Pippa firmly, "If you start to feel any worse, go home. I'll look after the phones. I don't have any appointments until tomorrow, so I can stay in and catch up with some paperwork."

"Thanks, Pippa, but I think I can manage," said Beth gamely.

Beth's brave words proved rather optimistic though and by eleven o'clock she had admitted defeat and gone home, leaving Pippa to hold the fort.

Mike had been on the telephone to Ian, three times since that early morning call and Ian needed a break. So, in desperation, just before half past twelve, he went out leaving his mobile phone on charge.

He had decided a quick run would revive his spirits and replenish his store of patience and good humour. He knew Mike would calm down eventually and he did not want to hurt his brother's feelings as he was looking forward to them working together, but until the project got off the ground he knew Mike would remain edgy and in need of reassurance and there was nothing concrete Ian could do to help until that appointment with Mike's bank which had been arranged for Wednesday afternoon, so making himself unavailable was the only option.

While he was running towards the canal, Ian decided that lunch with Pippa would be a good idea if she was free, especially as it would keep him out of the house even longer, so he changed direction and he headed for the auction rooms instead.

Pippa, as it happened, was starving. Having made her magnanimous gesture to Beth, she was stuck in the office with nothing but a few stale biscuits to sustain her. She had tried ringing Ian to suggest that he brought some sandwiches with him and they ate them together in the office, but he was not answering either of his phones so she made herself a cup of coffee and hugged her stomach in an effort to stop it rumbling, knowing that she would now have to wait until James returned from his meeting before she could venture out for some food. Consequently, when Ian put his head round the office door a little while later, she welcomed him with heartfelt relief.

"Oh Ian, you don't know how *pleased* I am to see you," she said, giving him a beaming smile.

"Hello," said Ian, slightly startled at his reception. "All on your own?"

"Yes I am. Beth has a dreadful cold and has gone home. James is out at a meeting and I have to man the phones, but I haven't had a chance to buy any lunch. You couldn't possibly go out and get me a sandwich could you?"

"I can do much better than that," he said with a grin. "I haven't had my lunch either, so I could get myself one too, bring them both back here and we can have our lunch together. I'm hiding out from Mike and he wouldn't dream of looking for me here, so it suits me very well. What do you want me to get?"

"How about a tuna sandwich? The café over the road does some quite tasty ones," said Pippa and as an afterthought she added, "Oh, and a milkshake or orange juice or something would be good, I could do with a change from coffee."

Ian set off on his mercy mission and returned with a plastic bag laden with enough lunch for about four people, having added a few cakes and several packets of crisps to the order. He wasn't sure which crisps Pippa might like, so he had bought her a selection from which to choose.

"That didn't take you long, I thought there might have been a long queue at this time, I usually go earlier just in case. Oh good, you have bought some crisps too," she said delving into the carrier bag.

"Why are you hiding from Mike?" Pippa asked, taking an enormous bite out of her sandwich and proceeding to devour it with relish.

"He is in a state because nothing has been finalised yet and he's worried the whole deal will fall through before we have been to see the bank together. He couldn't get an appointment before Wednesday, so he is going to be uptight for another couple of days I'm afraid. I think Gaynor must have been out somewhere. She usually manages to rationalise things for him and that calms him down. Never mind Mike, what did James say about the bowl?"

"He liked it and is going to speak to some contacts about it; apparently, if he plays his cards right, Gran could be in for a very nice windfall, possibly a thousand pounds," she said and Ian was suitably impressed.

"That's another auction I will have to go to then. I'm getting quite interested in all the different things you can find at an auction and how much people are prepared to pay for them," he said.

They carried on chatting and fortunately they were only interrupted by the telephone once and then Ian remembered something he had been meaning to ask Pippa.

"I promised Garth and Chrissie that I would fix up a date for us to go round to their house one evening next week and I was wondering which evening would be best for you," he said.

"Any night really, but preferably not Tuesday," said Pippa, an avid Holby City fan. "I'm looking forward to meeting them both. Wednesday or Thursday perhaps, what night do you think?"

"Let's settle on Thursday then. I'll check with Garth and let you know later. I suppose I'd better get off now and let you get on with some work," said Ian reluctantly, checking his watch and seeing that it was well after two.

"Will I see you tonight?" asked Pippa eagerly. Ian agreed that he would be round at her flat in time for supper and having also agreed to hire a video on the way home for them to watch later, he parted from Pippa with a quick hug and a kiss.

Alone again and with only her thoughts for company, Pippa stared blankly into space, a dreamy look on her face. A quote from her schooldays appeared on the empty screen of her mind.

Familiar acts are beautiful through love.

Where had it come from she mused, one of the Poets for sure. Byron? Shelley? Yes, definitely Shelley. It was true, eating a very ordinary lunch of a few sandwiches and some crisps had been turned into a beautiful event by sharing them with her Ian and lunchtime had passed by all too fleetingly.

This delightful train of thought was brought to an abrupt end by the shrill ringing of the telephone. Pippa dragged herself reluctantly out of her romantic haze and down to earth with a bump as she picked up the receiver and, now back in professional mode, she answered the caller airily with, "Good afternoon, McFarlanes."

8

For Mike, Wednesday afternoon was a long time coming but eventually and inevitably, it arrived and the two brothers both suited and booted, were sitting at the bank waiting for their meeting.

"Who are we seeing?" asked Ian. He had brought a file full of papers with him, amongst which were his cv and a list of all his qualifications, plus his passport, birth certificate and his driving licence. He wasn't exactly sure what was required of him, but he was not one to leave anything to chance, so he had brought every official document he could think of to cover all eventualities.

"The small business adviser," said Mike tersely. He was clutching his briefcase on his knees very tightly as if it contained the Crown Jewels rather than the preliminary plans for his new housing development, but he seemed fairly calm and for that, Ian was truly grateful.

An affable young man in a very sharp suit, shiny shoes and with a smile to match opened a door near the waiting area and called them in.

"What will he know," said Mike dismissively under his breath to Ian. "He looks as if he should still be at school."

"Give him a chance, Mike, appearances can be deceptive," said Ian in reply and followed Mike into the room.

Forty minutes later, the plans approved, the papers signed, the money assured and finally given the go-ahead, Mike and Ian, in turn, shook hands with the well-informed erstwhile schoolboy and drove back to Mike's house to tell Gaynor the good news.

Mike was elated.

"Well, no going back now," he said. "We've done it at last and we can speak to the agent, pay our deposit and start clearing the site."

"Good. I'm looking forward to getting stuck in," replied Ian with genuine enthusiasm. "We just have to thrash out a contract for me so there aren't any arguments later."

"You are absolutely right," said his brother as they drew into his drive. "We'll go and sort it out straight away."

They got out of the car and Mike opened the front door, calling out loudly as he did so, "Are you in Gaye?"

"I'm in here Mike," said an uncharacteristically feeble, but familiar voice from the sitting room. "I have a shocking headache, so I'm just having a sit down."

Mike popped his head round the sitting room door to find Gaye sitting quietly on the settee with her head back against the cushions and her eyes closed.

"Well, I have some news that will make you feel better. The bank has okayed everything, so Ian and I are going to discuss his contract now, in the office."

"That's great news, Mike," said Gaynor feebly without opening her eyes. "I am really pleased it all worked out. Could you make me a cup of tea before you disappear? I'm sure if I sit here quietly for a bit longer the headache will go away." Mike said he would and left her in peace.

It was Ian, in fact, who actually made the tea and took it through to Gaynor, then he shut the sitting room door noiselessly behind him and went into the office to join Mike, carrying two more mugs of tea with him to oil the wheels of their negotiations.

"Have I got time to ring Pippa before we start? I said I would let her know how we got on," said Ian.

"Of course, go ahead. I have to find my calculator first anyhow," said Mike and with that he disappeared to another part of the house, grumbling to himself about people moving his things about when he was not looking.

Pippa had just finished dealing with an awkward customer who, dissatisfied with Pippa's valuation of some very mediocre pieces of jewellery, was indignantly gathering them all up again into her bag and declaring that she would get someone else to value her jewellery, insinuating that Pippa did not know what on earth she was talking about. Her parting shot was, "It *must* be worth more than that; most of it is over fifty years old!"

Pippa saw her politely out of the door and shut it quickly. The sun was shining outside, but Pippa felt shivery and she went to look for her jacket. It was at that precise moment that Ian's call came through on her mobile and she answered it at once.

"Deal done," he said leaving her to guess as to his meaning.

"Sorry?" said Pippa, still feeling a bit put out by her last encounter and not really concentrating.

"Signed, sealed and delivered," he added cryptically. The penny finally dropped.

"Oh, good. You mean Mike's master plan, I suppose," she replied. "Come round tonight and tell me all about it. Is it extra cold today, or is it me?" Pippa asked.

"It isn't cold here, but then there *is* a lot of hot air around as you can imagine," said Ian wickedly and on hearing Mike in the passageway, he ended the call with a quick, "See you tonight."

Ian didn't manage to leave Mike and Gaynor's before six o'clock, but at least the two brothers had managed to sort out a contract to each other's satisfaction and Mike was now in a position to discuss every detail with his solicitor.

Gaynor's headache had not improved and she had gone up to bed early, which was not like her at all. She told Mike she thought she must have a temperature and he in turn thought that bed was probably the best place for her and now that he had settled his affairs, he was quite happy to cluck over her with hot water bottles, special hot toddies and the like. Ian went home to change out of his suit, then set off for Pippa's, only to discover that she too had a temperature and a raging sore throat.

"I think I must have caught Beth's cold," she said, shivering as she spoke. "I hope she is back at work tomorrow, because I don't feel at all well."

"Let me make you some soup," said Ian kindly. "Have you taken some paracetamol?"

"Soup would be lovely, thanks Ian. Yes I took some before I left work. Do you mind if I have a hot bath first? Sorry to be a wimp."

"Don't be silly, it is not your fault you don't feel well. Go and have your bath and I will deal with the soup." Pippa didn't argue and went off to try and warm up.

The next morning Ian rang Pippa to see how she was feeling, but her reply alarmed him very much.

"Pretty grim," said a very gruff voice that he didn't recognise as Pippa's. "I have been tossing and turning all night. I can't possibly go into work. My head aches and I can hardly swallow."

"Is there anything you need?" Ian asked, "I have to call at the supermarket today anyway."

"Not really. You had better stay away Ian. You don't want to catch this, whatever it is."

"I have a better idea. What if you wrapped yourself up and I collected you in my car and brought you here? Then I could look after you properly," he said gently.

He suddenly felt it was very important that he looked after Pippa. He didn't like to think of her alone and feeling wretched and he wasn't familiar with her flat. He knew he could do the looking after, better at his house. After a little more persuasion, Pippa agreed and he arranged to pick her up after he had been shopping. It would seem there was some sort of bug about and Ian thought he had better ring Mike to check on Gaynor.

"She is not too good I am afraid, mate," said Mike sounding unusually concerned. "Roaring temperature and now she is sneezing all over the place too. You had better steer well clear."

In the circumstances Ian thought he had better not tell Mike about Pippa staying with him, so he sent his love to Gaynor and left it at that.

Ian collected several patent cold and flu remedies from the supermarket, then some lemons and honey as his mother had been a great advocate of these for sore throats and coughs, then finally he filled up his basket with soup and a few other basics before setting off to rescue his damsel in distress.

She did look a sorry sight; pale face, dark rings round her eyes and when she opened her mouth, she could only talk in a raspy croak. Her hair was in plaits and she was wearing tracksuit bottoms and a thick jumper over her silk pyjamas and her black coat over the top of everything. Ian was not happy until he had her tucked up in bed and had dosed her with several spoonfuls of lemon and honey. Fortunately Pippa had not lost her sense of humour and now she was finally warm and comfortable, she told him he would have made an excellent Florence Nightingale, except for the stubble on his chin.

"Watch it," he retorted, "Or I will only feed you with stale bread and gruel. What did James say when you rang in?"

"He told me to make sure I was quite better before I went back to work," she croaked pathetically. "Apparently Beth is back in the office this morning, so he can manage for a while without me."

"Good," said Ian, sitting on the bed beside her. "Don't get better too soon though, I really like having you here," realising as he said those last few words, just how true they were. It felt so natural to have Pippa staying at his house with him. His thoughts then went on down the line of her moving in with him permanently, but he rejected that idea straight away as to him this seemed an impossible dream at present. But it was a persistent little thought, it had occurred to him before and it would occur to him again. It had no intention of staying rejected for long.

Had he but known it, a similar thought had occurred to Pippa, but hers involved a proposal first and she was just waiting to be asked.

9

Over the next couple of days, Pippa's temperature burned itself out and she began to improve. Then on Sunday morning she received a telephone call which made her feel even better still.

Isobel and Adrian had spoken to Will Grace about the incident at the waterfall and had asked him to let them know when Dollie had her puppies, so that they could tell Pippa. The call had come late on Saturday night and Isobel had decided to leave it until the Sunday morning to ring her daughter.

Pippa was sitting up in bed when her mobile rang, watching early morning television and waiting for Ian, who had insisted she had breakfast in bed just one more time. Pippa had discovered that she quite liked all this attention and Ian had discovered that he quite liked providing it. In fact they were both thinking how nice it would be if Pippa didn't have to go back to her flat, but neither one of them felt they could say so to the other; Pippa because she did not want to appear too pushy and Ian because he was worried she would think it was too soon.

As Ian walked up the stairs with their breakfast on a tray, he could hear Pippa's voice and he realised that she was talking on her phone.

"How many, Mum?"

"Are you all right, Pippa? You sound a bit croaky," said Isobel across the ether from her warm kitchen in Hardale.

"Much better now thanks, I have had a really horrid feverish cold and sore throat, but Ian has been looking after me. Never mind about me, I'm on the mend. How many puppies did you say?"

"Four," repeated her mother and she then went on to explain that one of the puppies had been stillborn, which left only two bitches and a dog in the litter.

"Hang on, I will just tell Ian." Pippa held the phone away from her ear and relayed this information to Ian who had just appeared with the tray.

"What a relief. Much better news than I had expected," he said, pleased Dollie had only lost one of the puppies.

"That's really good news, Mum," said Pippa, clearing her throat and picking up the threads of her conversation with her mother. "We are both very relieved. I'm so glad you let me know."

"Have you had to stay off work, Pippa?" Isobel asked, concerned, knowing that her daughter very rarely called in sick.

"Yes, but only for a couple of days," said Pippa, trying not to cough. "As I told you before, I feel much better now and I'm going back to work tomorrow."

"That's good. I'm going round to see the puppies later on in the week, so I will ring you again when I've been," said Isobel and with a few more words of advice about wrapping up warm and other motherly strictures, she left Pippa to her breakfast.

The cold virus, not content with Beth, Gaynor and Pippa, had claimed another victim and over the weekend, Mike too had succumbed.

Gaynor was well on the mend by then, which was fortunate because Mike was a very bad patient and by the time Monday morning dawned, she was stir-crazy and rang Ian to see if he would call round to keep Mike company for a bit while she went out.

As Pippa had returned to her flat on Sunday night and was back at work on Monday as she had told her mother she would be, Ian was at a loose end and consequently he was happy to give Gaynor a hand. He set off for their house, buying some football magazines on the way and the biggest bottle of Lucozade he could find.

Gaynor let him in with a relieved smile and lost no time in letting herself, out.

"I will probably be a couple of hours," she called from the front path. "I will bring back some lunch with me. Good luck, he's not in a very good mood!"

Ian took that on board and then taking a deep breath he walked up the stairs. He found his brother in his bedroom in his king-size bed wrapped up in a pair of pyjamas decorated with swaying palm trees, the bedside table littered with medicine of all kinds from throat lozenges to anti-inflammatory tablets and cough linctus. Mike's face was flushed and he looked very sorry for himself.

"What are *you* doing here?" was his lukewarm welcome. "Is Gaye around? I need another drink. This throat feels like the bottom of a birdcage."

"Gaynor has gone out for a bit and I have bought you some Lucozade," said Ian calmly.

"Never touch the stuff," said Mike crossly, "I need some blackcurrant squash. It's the only thing that makes me feel any better and I'm sure I need some more paracetamol."

"Right. I'll go and look for the squash," said Ian evenly, "In the meantime, here are some things for you to read," he said and he handed over the folded-up magazines.

"Oh thanks, I haven't seen these," said Mike, briefly scanning the contents of each one, "And Ian, my hot water bottle has gone cold," he moaned plaintively, but Mike was talking to thin air as Ian had already escaped downstairs and was busy searching the kitchen cupboards for blackcurrant squash and a glass in which to put it.

Having eventually succeeded in his quest, Ian took the squash upstairs and sat down beside the bed to have a chat with the invalid.

"I haven't told you about my weekend away properly yet, have I? Guess what car Pippa's mum drives," said Ian.

"I don't know," said Mike a little grumpily. He was not really in the mood for playing guessing games. "Something smart I expect."

"Not at all. It is in fact a forty year old Morris Traveller." Mike perked up immediately.

"What a coincidence. I bet she has trouble getting it started when the weather's cold," he said smugly.

"Actually she *was* having a bit of bother with it, but those Sunday afternoons with Dad weren't wasted as I managed to fix it for her," said Ian with, it has to be said, a certain amount of pride.

"Trust you," said Mike with the ghost of a smile.

"Then there was the dog and the waterfall," said Ian tantalizingly. Mike was at last showing a bit of interest and seemed to have forgotten his sore throat for the moment, so Ian made the most of it and padded out his heroic adventure, including in his tale the latest news about the safe arrival of most of the puppies.

"You were both lucky not to have broken anything climbing down there in the dark. I know you have always wanted a dog, but give me my fish any time," said Mike, pointing in the general direction of the ornamental pond in his back garden. "They don't need to be taken out for walks and they don't whine, bark or slobber either. Come to think of it, any mess they make goes into the bottom of the pond so that's easily sorted too."

Mike was really letting his enthusiasm for all things piscicultural run away with him. Then yet another thought occurred to him and he pulled himself up on his elbows, saying with a glint in his eye, "And what's more, they certainly wouldn't need rescuing from some random waterfall either." His triumph was complete.

This made them both laugh a lot and when Gaynor opened the bedroom door five minutes later, she was delighted to see that her husband was in much better spirits.

"Hello you two, I could hear you laughing from outside. What's the joke?"

Mike lay back against his pillows, looking very pleased with himself.

"Ian has been telling me about his weekend away. I'll explain later," he said. "What's for lunch, Gaye? I feel quite hungry now."

"That's good, you must be on the mend then. I thought we would have omelettes. Is that all right with you Ian?"

"That will be fine thanks, a rare treat even. I love omelettes but I'm not much good at making them myself," said Ian.

"Omelettes it is then. How *are* you feeling now Mike?" Gaynor asked, hoping for a positive reply.

"Much better, Gaye, I think my temperature has gone. Ian has been taking my mind off things. Actually,

I think I'll get up after lunch," finished her husband, sounding much less miserable than he had done for the last few days and much more like himself. Gaynor left to sort out lunch with a spring in her step and she thanked her lucky stars that the patient was improving at last.

10

Mike ended up staying at home for a whole week as he had developed a hacking cough and for once he had allowed Gaynor to put her foot down and keep him out of the March winds and away from Chisholm Construction until the weather had improved a bit. After all, he still had his telephone and the computer to keep things moving along and his site manager, Eric, had been to visit him several times with updates on all his projects.

On the Thursday evening as arranged, Ian and Pippa went round to see Garth and Chrissie for supper.

"Chrissie wanted me to ask you if you had ever been to ballet classes, but I've only just remembered," said Ian as they waited for someone to answer the door.

"Not me," said Pippa ruefully. "My Dad always said I was as light on my feet as a baby elephant. I was much happier climbing trees, playing tennis or swimming," she added. At which point the door opened and Garth greeted them warmly and ushered them into his front room.

"Chrissie will be down in a minute, she is just checking on the boys. I expect Ian has told you that we have twin boys, Pippa? And by the way, I am delighted to meet you at last. Up until now, you have only been a shadowy and mysterious figure," said Garth with a smile.

"I think I quite like the idea of being mysterious," said Pippa, "But shadowy? With my hair? I don't think so," she said with a gurgle of laughter. "Yes, Ian did tell me about your boys, but I can't remember how old they are."

"Five at the last count and they have just started at school," replied their proud father. "Did you two have a good weekend up in Cumbria?"

"Yes thanks, really good," answered Ian. "It was quite eventful though and in my opinion, far too short."

The door opened then and Chrissie came in looking serene and very attractive in a floaty white blouse on top of a pair of faded jeans, her medium-length straight black hair loose around her shoulders.

"Hello everyone, sorry I am late. You must be Pippa," she said, walking towards Pippa and holding out her hand with a smile. "Garth and I have been longing to meet you. I hope you haven't told Garth all the news before I got here," she added. "I hate being left out and he never remembers all the interesting bits."

"It's all right, you haven't missed anything yet," said Ian.

"Right, well hold fire while I get us some drinks. The curry is not quite ready yet," she said and immediately proceeded to find out what everyone wanted. Garth waited until she had asked everyone and then volunteered to go off and fetch the drinks himself while Chrissie sat down to hear all about their weekend away. It was the third time the story had been told and Ian and Pippa between them had it down to a fine art, managing to leave out nothing.

When it was finally time to eat, they all moved into the large farmhouse style kitchen, which was now filled with the tantalising scents of the Far East and they sat down around the circular pine table to enjoy Chrissie's famous rogan josh, to talk, drink, eat and talk some more.

Ian was thinking how good it was to see Pippa getting on so well with two of his favourite people. He was also beginning to think that not only would he like her to move in with him but he would like to put their relationship on a more formal footing too. He had never considered marrying anyone before and if he were completely honest, he found this quite a scary thought, but not scary enough to put him off the idea altogether and while they were all talking, he was wondering about an appropriate time to ask her. Then an unsettling thought occurred to him. Would an independent girl like Pippa want to be married at all? That stumped him, but fortunately for Ian and his tortured mental thought processes, Garth interrupted his reverie with, "Ian, I forgot to tell you that I have some news about Nimbus."

"Oh, what's happened?" Ian asked, all ears. "Don't forget Pippa is just as interested as I am you know Garth, Tim is her brother after all."

"Sorry, I forgot for the moment, of course he is. Well Ian *and* Pippa," he carried on very precisely, making them all smile, "The band has just redone the CD and it sounds marvellous, so in a few weeks' time it will be released and then we'll see what Jo Public thinks about Nimbus."

"Thank you so much Garth, I expect Tim is delighted. I wonder why he hasn't told me all about it," said Pippa, slightly nonplussed.

"There is a very good reason for that," said Garth with a grin. "He doesn't know it himself as yet because I haven't been able to contact him."

"Why is that, I wonder?" Pippa asked herself out loud, her mouth taking on an uncharacteristic pout. Suddenly, the clouds of confusion lifted, and she said, "Of course, he always goes away at this time of year with buddies from his university days. I won't say anything, I will let him ring me with the news," she finished magnanimously, mindful that it was Tim's news to tell.

"Talking of brothers, did you decide to take up Mike's job offer in the end?" Chrissie asked Ian.

"Yes I did and as I speak, I am pleased to say that it's all systems go. Mike is laid up with a bad cold at the moment, which doesn't stop him ringing me with monotonous regularity," he said with a resigned smile, "But come next week I don't suppose my feet will touch the ground. I'm quite looking forward to it now. I've been twiddling my thumbs for far too long."

Then as Garth, Chrissie and Pippa discussed present and past jobs between themselves and Pippa put Chrissie right as to her dancing abilities, Ian kept out of the loop because he wanted some more time to think about his future with Pippa now he had finally started to unravel the woolly tangle of his thoughts.

He made the decision that asking her to marry him was not on the cards as he did not want to make a fool of himself by risking rejection, so he would ask her to move in with him first and then he would have time to do some research into her views on marriage. After all, this idea had been floating around in his head since as far back as Valentine's Day if he was entirely truthful and now he just wanted to get on and do it. Satisfied that he had finally hit on the right strategy, Ian made up his mind that he was going to expedite the moving in together scenario. All that was left for him to decide on now, were the right words and the right time.

"It's a good job we haven't made any definite arrangements for our Italian trip with this job taking off," said Ian as he and Pippa were sitting in a cosy country pub having a quiet drink on the following Sunday night.

"It doesn't matter when we go," said Pippa reasonably. "The summer will be just as much fun. It will give us longer to do our planning too. I'm still having the time off over Easter though, because I have already arranged that with James."

Then Pippa opened her bag and took out a crumpled pink envelope with her name and address written on it in a tortuous childish script and handed it to Ian.

"I thought you might like to see this letter, Ian. It came in the post yesterday," she said.

He took the envelope from her hand and looked at it carefully. The postmark gave him no clues as to where it might have come from as only two of the letters from the franking were decipherable, so he asked Pippa directly, "Who is it from?"

"Open it and see," she replied enigmatically.

Ian took out the single rather grubby sheet of inexpertly folded up paper from inside the envelope and unfolded it to reveal the message. It read,

Dear Miss Flynn,

Thank you, thank you and thank you, for saving our Dollie. She is fine now.

From Rachel, Lucy and Fred.

P.S. Her puppies are very well too.

The writing was surrounded by pictures of little brown dogs with slightly curious faces, lopsided ears and crooked legs, but each one with a tail wagging merrily.

"Ah, that's nice," said Ian with a smile. "They've taken a lot of trouble over it. The puppies must be a week old now. I wonder what they have called them?"

"I can't imagine, but you know what children are like, they will probably choose names like Fluffy, Spot, or Cheeky," said Pippa pulling a face, then she added as an afterthought, "I had a hamster once that I called 'Nibbles'."

"How about Mixture, Jelly or even Liquorice?" suggested Ian with a laugh joining in the joke. Pippa laughed too, but said she thought that would be a bit too sophisticated for children to dream up. Then, completely changing the subject, she asked Ian, "Are you coming to the auction preview next week? There is a fabulous Chinese robe I want you to see. I'm thinking of bidding on it as I am sure Mum would love it and I can just see her swanning around the house wearing it but I'd like to know what you think first. If I'm lucky, it shouldn't be too expensive."

"Yes, I did think I might come and have a look before the auction," said Ian. "Who knows, there might be something *I* would like to buy. I'm definitely coming on Friday anyway as I want to know how the bidding goes on your gran's bowl."

Talking about all these things with her made him even more certain that the decision he had made on Thursday night had been the right one and that he needed Pippa to move in with him as soon as possible. He wanted her to be part of his day-to-day life, he wanted to include her in everything he did and he also knew that he wouldn't rest until he had asked her. Perhaps it was thinking back to Cumbria and how happy they had been there and how lovely her family was, that had clinched it.

In that split second everything became clear to him, he was going to ask her to move in with him this coming weekend. On Saturday night, over a nice meal? No, that didn't feel right ... after the auction? Yes, that was it, he knew exactly what he was going to do and it was so obvious now, that he couldn't understand why he hadn't thought of it before. As he had concluded the other day, the marrying thing could wait; getting her to move in with him was the first step along the way and he finally knew just where and how to take it.

Unfortunately Pippa was completely unaware of Ian's plans and when she stayed at his house again that night she found herself wishing, not for the first, second or even third time, that he would ask her to marry him and move in with him permanently. She had already decided that she would prefer to be there with him and rent out her flat than the other way round. She hated having to go back to her flat after their outings and hated watching him leave to return to his house even more, but she was not going to suggest such a thing herself.

It was important to her that Ian made the first move. The suggestion had to come from him and much as it went against the grain, she realised that she was just going to have to be patient, however long it took.

11

Ian had been right about Mike and the speed with which he would get things moving on their joint project once he was back at work. He had spoken to the agents from his sickbed and had the whole deal sewn up. Contracts had already been exchanged and a deposit paid, so the next step was to discuss the site layout, to which end Ian and Mike had made several site visits and had set up various meetings with Architects and Planners.

Consequently it was Thursday before Ian managed to find a couple of hours to himself during the working day, although he had managed to see Pippa every evening in between and he grabbed them greedily, then headed for the auction rooms before he could get waylaid by his brother.

As ever before an auction, the hall was bursting at the seams with a colourful and eclectic mix of furniture, china, jewellery and paintings, not to mention the usual bric-a-brac and a few books. When he arrived, there was a steady stream of visitors walking round the hall, checking their brochures and ticking off the items in which they were interested. Edith's bowl had pride of place standing alone on the top of a well-polished upright piano and Ian went across to admire it. It was then that he heard the voice at his shoulder.

"Here you are at last," said Pippa, whose voice it was.

"Hello Pippa. It's really buzzing in here today."

"It always is on the last day of viewing before a sale. Gran's bowl looks good, doesn't it?"

"Yes, it certainly catches the eye," said Ian supportively. "Where is that Chinese robe you were telling me about?"

"Round here," said Pippa, taking his hand and leading him off.

"There," she said, pointing to the gorgeously embroidered garment displayed on a hanger high up on the wall above the shelves of china. Ian could see why Pippa liked the robe so much and he was as taken as she was by the intricate design and glowing colours.

"You're right. I can definitely see your Mum wearing that," he agreed warmly. "You have to get it for her."

"I'll try, but I'm not going over a hundred pounds," she said firmly. "I really wanted to give it to her for her birthday next week though, so if I don't get it I will have to think of something else in a hurry."

"I could chip in if you like," said Ian helpfully. "It would be a shame to lose it. What do you think?"

"OK, if you want to, we'll see how it goes," replied Pippa. "Is there anything you fancy, Ian? Apart from me of course," she said coquettishly, fluttering her eyelashes at him in an exaggerated fashion.

"That goes without saying, as well you know," he said with a smile and then he added, "I haven't been able to have a proper look round yet."

"I'll leave you to it then. Come and see me before you go," she said and with that Pippa disappeared into the office.

Ian spent some time browsing and nothing much caught his eye until he noticed a small green vase in amongst a display of cut glass. It wasn't very big, but what attracted him to it was the sheep in the snow painted on one side. It said 'Hardale' to him without a doubt and he had to have it.

He found Pippa in the office, sitting down at the computer, standing in for Beth who had gone out for lunch.

"I have found something I'd like," said Ian eagerly.

"What is it? Is it one of those watercolours?"

"No, actually it's a small green vase with sheep on it," he said, thinking to himself how mundane it sounded, described like that.

"Lot 290? That is a Doulton vase," she said, scrolling through the list of lots on the computer. "I expect it will go for about four hundred pounds. It's a bit pricey," she said doubtfully.

"I am prepared to pay that much," said Ian, digging his heels in. "I expect you think this sounds a bit pathetic, but I like it because it reminds me of our weekend at the Killingbeck Ridge."

"Not at all," she said indignantly, "I think that's the *best* reason for buying something here. It has to have some meaning for you, not just be for investment purposes," said Pippa thinking what a lovely man he was and how fortunate she was to have found such a sensitive partner. Ian was a one-off and he was hers.

"It should come up at about twelve o'clock. Can you get here for then?" she asked.

"Yes, I'm sure I can. What number is the bowl?"

"Lot 414, so it won't be far behind your vase."

"Right, I'll make sure I'm here for both of them," he said. "Sorry Pippa, but much as I love your company, I have to get off now because Mike has an appointment with the Planners this afternoon and he wants me to go with him."

"I'll see you later then. Don't forget I am cooking tonight," said Pippa as she gave him a quick kiss goodbye.

Ian had been guilty of a bit of subterfuge and he had not told Pippa the whole truth when he had said he was going to a meeting with Mike. He *was* meeting Mike, but not until half past three, there was another job he had to do first before he joined Mike at the council offices and to him it was a much more important one. Ian didn't want Pippa to know what he was up to, so he wandered nonchalantly out of the auction rooms as if he had all day, but the second his feet touched the pavement outside, he set off walking down the high street at a brisk pace until he reached his goal. This was a small old-fashioned cobbler's shop tucked neatly away in a small side street between an estate agent's office and a high-class boutique selling designer label clothes.

One side of the narrow shop window was completely taken up with a display of leather purses and shoelaces and the other side by a stand of key fobs plus some dog identification discs. On the adjacent wall was a shelf neatly stacked with tins full of shoe polish in every conceivable colour and a rack of shoehorns. As Ian walked in through the door he felt as if he had stepped back in time. A powerful smell of strong glue mixed with raw leather pervaded the air and a bell hidden under the doormat jangled loudly but it was only just audible above the whirring and grinding of a buffing machine that seemed to him to be the nerve centre of this secret world.

A solitary man perched on a high stool mending shoes, looked up at Ian for a moment and then carried on with his work as his assistant, who was wearing a green stripy overall and a very cheery smile, appeared from behind some rainbow hued ribbons of plastic that were suspended from a doorway at the back of the shop, leaving them to sway in the breeze behind her as she moved forward to serve Ian.

"Good afternoon," she said. "How may I help you?"

"I need a spare key cut," he said taking the front door key he had brought with him out of his pocket and handing it over the counter to be copied.

"Let me just check that I have the right blank," she said taking it from him and scrutinising it carefully before quickly scanning her stock of shiny virgin keys. "Yes, that's fine I can do it straight away. It should only take me about five minutes," she said pleasantly. "Do you want to collect it later, or will you wait?"

"I'll wait, thanks if you don't mind," said Ian and, choosing one of the white plastic chairs lined up on either side of the entrance door for the convenience of customers needing a quick repair of shoes they were actually wearing, he settled himself down to watch the work in progress.

12

Ivy Ellison did not feel at all well. Earlier on in the week she had caught a cold which had now ended up on her chest and despite the best efforts of Olbas Oil, she could not shift it. Every movement caused her pain and breathing was an uphill struggle. She had no option but to stay in bed where she had taken herself off to after lunch, because try as she might, she did not have the strength to move.

Her daughter Claire, was unfortunately not due to visit until the weekend; if only she could reach the phone. The mobile her daughter had bought her was still in its box because she couldn't fathom how to use it. She had meant to ask Ian to show her, but now he was working with his brother and had found that nice Pippa, she did not see him as often these days, even though he only lived next door to her and she certainly did not want to make a nuisance of herself by dropping round to see him every five minutes. Eventually Ivy drifted off into a fitful sleep, her breathing laboured, hoping against hope that she would feel much better in the morning.

Ian arrived back home after his meeting with Mike and the Planners and noticed straight away that Ivy's house was in darkness. She rarely went out in the evenings and when he had been round to see his old neighbour on his return from the Lake District, she had not mentioned any holidays she might be taking. It was altogether very odd, he thought to himself as he opened his front door, unless she had gone out with some of her church friends, which was a possibility. He decided to go round next door on his way out to Pippa's, just to check for his own peace of mind that all was well.

So an hour later, freshly showered and having changed out of his working clothes and into a casual shirt and trousers, Ian took Ivy's spare key from the pot on his hall table and walked up her path. He opened the door and called out her name, but there was no reply. He switched on the sitting room light and had a quick look round. It all seemed fine. For some unknown reason, he was drawn up the stairs and when he reached the landing he could hear her rasping breaths and he knew straight away that something was very wrong.

He switched on her bedroom light, at the same time saying quietly and calmly, but with a feeling closely akin to panic in the pit of his stomach, "Hello Mrs E., it's Ian." The air was thick with the smell of camphor and cough mixture and Ian noticed that the curtains had not been drawn. Then he saw Ivy lying unresponsive in her bed with its sumptuous red-silk counterpane, her cheeks in contrast as pale as could be, beads of perspiration glistening on her forehead.

"Ivy, Ivy," he said urgently. She continued to breathe heavily, but did not open her eyes. He tried shaking her arm but there was still no reaction. Finally he realised that he would have to call for help and he reached for his phone. First he dialled 999 and asked for an ambulance and then he rang Pippa to let her know that he would not be joining her for supper after all and while he waited for the ambulance to arrive, he walked up and down the room, his gaze never wavering from the inert form in the bed.

Pippa sat down dejectedly on one of her kitchen stools. Ian's call had thrown her completely. She had only met Ivy recently, but she thought she was a lovely old lady and one with a bit of a character, very much like her gran. She knew Ian was very fond of her and that they had known each other forever. It was worrying that he had sounded so concerned as he wasn't one to flap as a general rule and she knew then that it must be serious.

Fortunately from her point of view, she had only planned to cook pasta for their supper and that would keep for another evening and she suddenly realised that she wasn't really hungry any more anyway, so she made herself some cheese on toast and sat down to eat it while she waited for another news bulletin from Ian, to let her know how Ivy was doing.

As she sat there, her mind skipping from one thought to another, her eyes fell upon her grandmother's parting gift. She had put the briefcase on a shelf in the kitchen intending to look at it when she had a spare moment, but so far that moment had not presented itself … until now and if the truth were told, with one thing and another, she had forgotten all about it. Now she had an excellent opportunity to see what secrets it was keeping hidden.

Pleased to have something to occupy her mind, Pippa gathered it up from the shelf and carried it into her lounge where she sat down on a comfortable chair and rested the briefcase on her knees. She undid the buckles, then the catch and started to plough through the contents. It was full of yellow-ish pieces of tissue paper all different shapes and sizes, with strange markings on them and then various sheets of paper covered in sketches of clothes, some of them of children's outfits, dresses, skirts, coats, dungarees and also amongst them several wedding gowns. Then it clicked. These were the patterns Edith had used to make Isobel's clothes all those years ago.

Pippa tipped the whole lot out onto the floor and on rifling through the sketches a bit more thoroughly she discovered to her surprise that a significant number of them were of wedding dresses, complete with trains and veils. Some were very fussy with ruffles and fancy bodices and others were just simple or streamlined gowns. All were well-drawn, exquisite designs and without exception very stylish. Her grandmother definitely had a hidden talent. Who had she designed these dresses for? What was the story behind them? There was, of course, only one person who could answer these questions, so Pippa decided to ring Edith and solve the intriguing mystery straight away.

Using her landline in case Ian rang her mobile, she dialled the number and waited.

"Hello Gran," she said cheerfully when her grandmother finally answered the telephone.

"Is that you Pippa?" came the reply. "I have been waiting for you to call. I expect you have finally had a look in that case at last."

"How did you know that was why I was ringing?" Pippa asked, amused at her grandmother's perspicacity. "Of course," she added with a laugh, "You must have read it in your tealeaves."

"Why no, not at all. I knew that once you had had a chance to look in the case you would want to know why I gave it to you," replied her gran rather tartly.

"Yes, I do want to know," said Pippa contritely. "What really fascinates me is why there are so many wedding dress designs. I am guessing the other patterns and things were for Mum's clothes when she was little, but she didn't even wear a formal wedding dress, so I have to admit I am somewhat baffled by it all."

"Well, Pippa, the truth is that I have always liked designing clothes and when your mum went off to college I had more time to do it. Some of those designs were used by my friends or their daughters, but a lot of them were intended for Isobel and when she decided on a more individual wedding outfit, I just put all my ideas away in that case with all the other patterns. She never knew about them," said Edith a little breathlessly.

"When I met your Ian," she went on in her gentle lilt, "I felt sure that you and he would settle down together and that one day you would marry and might like to use one of my original designs for *your* wedding dress because I could see that you have a more traditional approach to life than your mum. That is why I gave you the case for safekeeping as I don't know how much longer I will be here and I didn't want all my sketches to be just thrown away as so much scrap paper."

There was complete silence from Pippa's end of the phone. Being in an emotional frame of mind over Ivy, this tipped her over the edge and she wanted to compose herself before she answered her grandmother. She thought it was so sad that Edith had yearned to see her only daughter in a wedding dress designed by her, but had had the generosity of spirit not to make Isobel feel guilty for making her own choice. How well she knew Pippa, she *did* like more traditional styles of dress than her mother and the idea of walking down the aisle with Ian wearing a dress exclusively designed by her own grandmother held immense appeal for Pippa. Edith had been quite right.

"Pippa? Are you still there, lovey?" Edith tapped her phone and then she shook it. Perhaps she had been cut off. "Pippa?" Edith tried one last time.

"I'm still here, Gran," said Pippa quietly, brushing her tears away as she spoke. "You were right, I *do* like your ideas and if Ian ever gets round to asking me to marry him, I promise you I will be walking down the aisle in one of your designs."

Ian meanwhile, whilst being blissfully unaware of this very revealing conversation between Pippa and her grandmother, was now sitting on a very uncomfortable chair in a hospital corridor drinking what passed for a cup of coffee. Ivy had still not come round, but was being treated with oxygen and after several tests, had been declared to be suffering from double pneumonia. The next step he understood, was a large dose of intravenous antibiotics and a bed on a ward but this had still not been organised and Ian did not want to leave the old lady until she *was* safely tucked up in bed on a ward, as although the hospital had managed to contact Ivy's daughter Claire, she had not arrived at the hospital as yet and he was not going to leave Ivy there, all on her own.

It was eleven o'clock when he finally returned home and he phoned Pippa straight away.

She had gone to bed, but was not asleep when her phone rang and she was very relieved indeed, to hear that Ivy was in safe hands and receiving treatment.

"Can we go and visit her tomorrow evening?" she asked tentatively.

"I think I will try and go earlier than that, probably tomorrow morning, so if I'm not there when my vase comes up, could you bid for me? I'll go up to five hundred," said Ian in reply.

"It's the least I can do," said Pippa, glad to be able to help in a crisis. "Leave it with me."

13

"She didn't look too good, did she?" Mike asked Ian as they left the hospital together on Friday morning.

"Better than she looked yesterday," said Ian sounding relieved, but still feeling a bit worried. "What was it that nurse said, it will be a long haul to get her right again at her age? I told Claire that Pippa and I would visit her again tomorrow," he said and then he added rather bleakly, "It reminded me of Mum, seeing her lying there."

"I know," said Mike, patting his brother's shoulder kindly. "That's why I came with you this morning. When you rang me last night to tell me about Ivy, I knew it would give you a jolt when you visited her today. This is pneumonia though, not cancer like Mum. It's serious but Claire said the doctor told her he thought Ivy would make a good recovery eventually as she has no other medical problems apart from a bit of arthritis."

Ian nodded and then he looked at his watch.

"I'll have to get off to the auction now Mike, I told Pippa I would try and be there mid-morning. I hope I'm not too late for the items I am interested in."

"That's an excellent idea mate, it will take your mind off Ivy for a while," said Mike. "Why don't you take the rest of the day off? We haven't got a lot to do now until the site has been cleared properly and we hear back from the subcontractors."

"Thanks, I think I will if you're sure you don't need me for anything," said Ian and then, parting company with his brother, he trekked off to find his car which he had parked somewhere amidst the row upon row of other vehicles, all neatly lined up looking like an army of clones in the sprawling hospital car park. He could not for the life of him remember exactly where he had left his car and this made him think that the idea he had been mulling over of buying something a bit more unusual, was a good one, if only to make it easier to find in the future when it might be parked in a similarly oversized car park.

Eventually, after walking around aimlessly for several minutes, Ian recognised a tall sycamore tree that he had noticed when he had left the car earlier, as it seemed to him to have had an inordinate amount of leaf buds on its branches far too soon for the time of year and by scanning the adjacent rows of cars, he eventually located his own and could at long last set off for McFarlane & Sons to join Pippa at the auction.

The sale was in full swing when Ian finally arrived and he made a beeline for Pippa through the crowd of bidders to see what number James was up to and if the vase had come up for offers yet. She was standing by the office door and Ian noticed admiringly, that she wearing a very smart short black dress with her favourite black suede boots and had tied her burnished hair in a low ponytail resting on her shoulders. The earrings he had given her before their trip up to the Lakes, were glittering in her ears and Pippa was watching and listening to the proceedings very carefully, but as he walked towards her she noticed him coming and she felt her face break into a smile.

"I see you're wearing those boots again," he said in her ear, giving her a surreptitious kiss on the cheek.

"I haven't got any other decent ones and anyway they're so comfortable, but I have got my eye on a nice pair of grey ones. I'm just waiting for them to be reduced in the end of season sale," she whispered back to him. Then she asked him quietly, not wanting to disturb the many serious-faced bidders who were listening attentively to lots coming and going waiting for their chance to jump in and grab a bargain, "How is she, Ian?"

"Not too good, but the doctors are optimistic that she will pull through," he replied in a low voice. "I said we would go and see her tomorrow, I hope that's all right with you."

"Of course," said Pippa softly, keeping half an ear on the state of the bidding as they were talking. "Not long now until your vase. Here's your bidding number, you might as well do it yourself now you're here," she said and she handed Ian a piece of white card about six inches long and four inches wide, with the number 177 printed on it in black. Ian took the card and on seeing the number, he looked at Pippa and whispered to her excitedly, "Seven is my lucky number."

"Good," she whispered back, "Because I think your lot is next."

Sure enough, James had just brought his gavel down on a watercolour of children on a hillside picking berries which went for one hundred and seventy pounds and was in the throes of announcing, "Lot number 290 a Royal Doulton Vase, with sheep in the snow. A nice example here and I can start the bidding at two hundred pounds. Any advance on two hundred? Thank you two ten, two twenty, two thirty." Pippa touched Ian's arm.

"Wait a bit and then jump in," she advised quietly. The bidding was up to three hundred and fifty pounds and James' voice droned on.

"Three hundred and sixty anywhere? This is a nice example and well worth the money. Thank you, three hundred and sixty pounds in the corner."

Then Ian put up his hand, catching James's eye and he was in with the bidding.

"Three hundred and seventy I have. Any more bids? Three hundred and eighty." He looked again at Ian who felt his hand rising once more. "Three hundred and ninety pounds. That is three hundred and ninety pounds to the gentleman standing at the back. Going once, going twice, sold at three hundred and ninety pounds. Number please ... Erm, the right way round if at all possible," said James and a ripple of laughter went round the room. Ian, slightly red-faced, swiftly rectified his mistake and the auction, having stopped briefly for James to have a sip of water from the glass on his rostrum, carried on relentlessly with, "Lot 291 an old Jaques boxwood chess set in an oblong mahogany box. Who will start the bidding?"

Ian couldn't believe it. Had he just bought a vase at auction? He looked across at Pippa who was smiling broadly at him.

"I think I have just bought a vase," said Ian, a bit dazed.

"Yes, you really have, well done you. Let's go outside for a minute."

Ian followed Pippa outside the hall into the yard, which only had a few people milling round it now, either collecting their furniture, or having a sly smoke before they returned to the hall for some more of the action.

"Phew!" Ian exclaimed, taking a deep breath and feeling the very welcome cool breeze on his face. "I could get a taste for this bidding business, it was really quite exciting, especially as I ended up with something I really wanted. I can see now how people get carried away in the auction room."

"Yes," agreed Pippa. "But it's not so nice when someone else pips you to the post. I wonder what will happen with Gran's bowl. I think we have probably got about half an hour to wait. Will you have time to stay?"

"I have got all afternoon actually. Mike didn't need me, so I can stay as long as I like," replied Ian. "What happened with that oriental dressing gown thing?"

"It won't be up until about four o'clock," said Pippa, smiling at his inaccurate description of the Chinese robe.

"Shall I get us some lunch then? I can nip across to the café again," offered Ian helpfully.

"Let's wait until the bowl has had its moment of glory, that should be quite exciting and you might miss it if you go now. We've had two commission bids on it already and I know for a fact that there are a few people in the hall who are after it as well."

"Right, I'll go later then. Would you like to go out for a meal tonight, after you've finished? We haven't been out to eat for a while and we could both do with a night out."

"Do you know, I think I would. Can we go to The Ship again? I like it there," she said eagerly.

"Yes, I was thinking of The Ship. Anyway, we need to talk and there is something I want to ask you." Pippa was intrigued by Ian's last comment, but much to her dismay, someone came looking for her at that precise moment and she had to stifle her curiosity for the time being and return to the office to sort out a problem.

Ian walked back into the hall and found himself a seat to wait for lot 414 to be called. He was beginning to know his way about auctions and felt quite at ease sitting there looking round the hall, watching while the other star turns strutted their stuff and waiting for the Imari bowl to become top of the bill.

Pippa managed to come back into the auction hall just as James started the bidding on Edith's bowl, but the hall was packed and she could not reach Ian who was sitting in the middle of the throng.

"A Japanese Imari bowl in a very unusual design," began James enthusiastically. "I have several commission bids on this one, so I can start the bidding at eight hundred pounds. Eight hundred and twenty anywhere? Thank you. Eight hundred and twenty pounds. Eight hundred and forty? Eight hundred and forty, sixty, eighty ..." The bidding was going well at a smart pace and Ian, watching to see which hands were going up each time, saw that it had become a duel between a middle-aged lady wearing an expensive-looking leather jacket and several gold bracelets that jangled each time she waved her bidding number at James and a young man with shoulder length hair in shirtsleeves and a body warmer. James had reached a thousand pounds and the bidding was still going strong. At one thousand two hundred pounds, Ian was holding his breath, so it was fortunate that the bowl was finally sold at one thousand three hundred pounds and way over its estimate, to the well-heeled lady in the leather jacket. James banged his gavel down looking very pleased with himself and Ian turned round to see if he could catch Pippa's eye, but she had completely disappeared. Ian quickly scanned the crowd for that one familiar face and then realising that she must have left the room for some reason, he got up out of his seat and went to look for her.

Pippa had, in fact, gone outside to ring Edith with the good news and that was where Ian found her a few minutes later.

"I am just ringing Gran with the good news. She always takes ages to answer her phone … Oh! She's answering now," said Pippa excitedly. "Hello Gran, it's Pippa. Are you sitting down?"

"Whatever is the matter lovey? You sound in a bit of a state," said Edith on the other end of the phone feeling slightly alarmed, her usually mellifluous tones sounding rather staccato.

"It is good news, Gran. It's about your bowl."

"Well, what have you got to tell me? Did you sell it at a good price?"

"It went for an excellent price," said Pippa. "What do you think of one thousand three hundred pounds?"

"No!" exclaimed Edith, completely shocked. "Are you teasing me?"

"It is perfectly true, Gran. There was a lot of interest in it. Are you pleased?"

"I am more than pleased. I bet Dorrie didn't know it was worth that much, nor her money grabbing nephew either or he wouldn't have handed it over," said Edith forthrightly. "Thank you for sorting it out for me, Pippa. Just wait until I tell your Mum," she said with delight and after just a few more words along the same lines, Edith put the phone down.

"Another satisfied customer," laughed Pippa. "I think we could have our lunch now."

Only a few miles away from Edith, in The Old Schoolhouse, Isobel and Adrian had just finished *their* lunch and were setting off for a quick walk with the dogs and taking the opportunity to discuss Isobel's forthcoming birthday which was in six days' time.

A slightly exasperated Adrian tried to sum up what they had decided so far.

"So we have established that you don't want a big fuss and you can't think of anything particular you would like me to buy for you. Shall we go out for dinner then?" He asked, hoping that he had hit upon a satisfactory solution.

"I can't decide what I want to do," she said unhelpfully. "Since Pippa and Ian visited, I have felt a bit unsettled and it reminded me that we haven't seen Tim for ages."

"Right, in that case I know exactly what to do," said Adrian, delighted that he had now thought up what he considered to be the *perfect* answer to the problem.

"How about booking into that nice hotel near Linchester, I think it was called Roman Reach and having a few days away? We can invite Tim and Pippa to have a meal with us there on your birthday; oh yes, and Ian too. I like him and Pippa wouldn't want us to leave him out. How's that?"

"What a marvellous idea darling," said Isobel, her eyes shining. "It would be lovely to have us all together for once, I can't remember the last time we managed that and of course Ian must be included, they *are* a couple now you know. That is just the sort of present I would *love*," she said, giving his arm an affectionate squeeze.

"I'll sort it out as soon as we get back home," said Adrian, already making a mental note of the list of things he would have to arrange for everything to run smoothly and hoping against hope that Pippa and Tim would both be available on the right day.

Gaynor on the other hand, having just had a brief sandwich lunch with Mike, who on swallowing the last mouthful of his currant bun had now returned to the office, was upstairs in their bedroom, wrestling with the duvet cover.

In her early married life she had religiously changed their bed every Monday morning without fail until she had realised that she had come to dread Mondays simply because they meant the inevitable tussle with the recalcitrant bed linen, so now she changed the bed on a different day each week and that way it always came as a surprise to her and did not seem so much of a nightmare. While she was performing this irksome task, her mind was elsewhere. She was thinking about her family.

Her first thought was that Mike and Ian were getting along much better now they were working together. This gave her tremendous satisfaction, because having a happy husband made *her* life much more pleasant too. Less grumbling from Mike about Ian doing nothing with his life and great praise from Mike for Pippa who had put a smile on Ian's face at last and had made him venture out from his self-imposed shell, which was another added bonus for all of them.

To fill up her jug of happiness she had just had a call from her elder daughter Jane, to say that she was coming home from university in York for a few days to study before some important exams she was taking. Having her children at home made Gaynor very happy indeed. Wouldn't it be good if Susie decided to turn up too? Their beds were always made up in case one or other of them arrived out of the blue, so all she had left to do was fill up the freezer, top up the fridge and wait for the train from York to arrive at Linchester station.

Only the pillowcases to deal with now, giving her a few minutes to mull over Ian and Pippa's relationship. According to Mike, they had enjoyed their trip to Cumbria and she had noticed that since they had been back, they rarely spent an evening apart. Perhaps they would make it official and be getting married soon. Gaynor hoped so, as she loved weddings and it would mean a smart new outfit for her and lots of excitement too not to mention catching up with the distant members of the Chisholm family that Mike would energetically round up for the celebrations.

A wedding, she thought as she plumped up the clean, sweet-smelling pillows, would be just the thing to blow away their emotional cobwebs after all the sadness of her mother-in-law's death and the shock of Ivy Ellison's illness. Having paid the old lady a visit only that morning, shortly after Mike and Ian, Gaynor was satisfied that she was slowly beginning to improve and although it might take some time, she was sure Ivy would pull through.

With one last satisfied smoothing down of her freshly laundered duvet, Gaynor, having successfully finished her allotted task, left the bedroom to make her assault on the supermarket.

14

The auction was finally drawing to a close. Pippa had been lucky with the Chinese robe and Isobel's purported birthday present had been safely secured at the very reasonable price of ninety-five pounds, but she and Ian had only managed a very quick lunch and their 'chat' was still on schedule for their dinner date at The Ship later on that evening.

Ian, left to his own devices, had also bought an Edwardian mantel clock-cum-thermometer-cum-barometer in an oblong oak case as well as the little Doulton vase and he was now waiting in the queue in the office to pay the bill.

Beth checked the computer.

"One Doulton vase at three hundred and ninety pounds and one clock/barometer at two hundred. Is that right, Mr Chisholm?

"Yes, that's all," said Ian, thinking to himself that it was quite enough and wondering what Pippa would say to his second purchase. He had always liked barometers and he didn't have a clock apart from the alarm clock in his bedroom, so this particular one set in its oak case with accompanying instruments had spoken to him. She would probably think he was quite mad, but with three functions all in one case it was, he thought, a very good buy.

He settled up and went to wait for Pippa in the hall.

She reappeared ten minutes later and found him sitting in the empty hall, his purchases on the chair beside him.

"What have you got there?" she asked.

"I couldn't resist this one," said Ian. "I like barometers. I'm toying with the idea of collecting them actually," he added ruminatively. "This oak case appealed to me and I thought at two hundred pounds it was a very good buy." He looked at her slightly apprehensively, worried as to what her reaction might be, but she smiled back at him and then picked up his latest acquisition to examine it more carefully.

"Not a bad bargain," she said. "It's a good make and it seems to be in working order. The case is in excellent shape too," she added running her fingers over the wood to check for damage. "Where are you going to put it?"

"In the hall I expect," he said, glad that her reaction was so positive. "I'll have to make a special shelf to hold it though, I don't think it will fit on the hall table. Are you meeting me at The Ship, or shall I give you a lift?"

"I'll follow you later," said Pippa, "I haven't quite finished here yet."

"O.K. I'll be there by seven," said Ian and took himself and his purchases off home.

As usual, he arrived at The Ship before Pippa and was waiting for her when she finally appeared. He had already booked a table for seven thirty hoping that she would manage to get there by then and checked his pocket surreptitiously one last time for the brand new key while he watched the door.

Pippa still had no inkling of what he had in store for her and when she arrived at twenty past seven she sat down heavily on the seat beside him saying wearily, "Thank goodness that's over for another month."

"I've booked the table for seven thirty, said Ian. "Would you like a drink first?"

"Yes please," said Pippa. "A gin and tonic I think, thanks."

When he returned with her drink, she thanked him and swallowed a generous mouthful of her restorative and then turned to him with a satisfied sigh.

"Ah, that's better," she said. "I think you wanted to tell me something earlier on Ian, before I got sidetracked, what's the problem?"

"There isn't one. Well, I *hope* not. I just thought it was time we had a chat about the future, that's all," said Ian and then he went quiet.

Pippa's heart turned over and her fatigue left her in a flash. Was he going to propose? She had imagined this scenario so many times before in her imagination; was he going to get down on one knee? Had he bought her a ring? A myriad of questions jostled together in her brain, but outwardly she appeared perfectly calm while she waited expectantly to see what he was going to say next.

"I wondered if you might consider moving in with me," he said all of a sudden. "I've got plenty of room and it would save us a lot of time going backwards and forwards between my house and your flat if you did. We would save money on petrol and food," he gabbled on, conscious of the fact that this wasn't coming out quite right . Now it was Pippa's turn to become silent and she was looking at him with an inscrutable expression on her face saying nothing, because Ian's words were echoing round and round in her head, '*consider* moving in with me', 'consider *moving in* with me', 'consider moving in *with me*'. Then Ian played his trump card.

"Basically, Pippa, I love it when you stay at my house. Everywhere seems terribly empty when you leave and all this to-ing and fro-ing is becoming ridiculous." Then he stopped and looked at her appealingly, waiting to see what she would make of his soul-baring performance.

If truth were told, Pippa was completely taken aback at Ian's suggestion and its timing and she couldn't understand what had instigated it. She had thought, or at least *hoped* that a proposal might have been a possibility at some stage in their relationship because marriage was to her the gold standard, but offering to share his home with her straight away and so early on in their relationship without an engagement first, was rather unexpected and she thought rather out of character for the Ian she had come to know and love.

Her antennae had not even picked up a hint of what was going on in his mind and while she had of course been hoping that he would ask her to move in with him eventually, she had thought it would only be *after* he had asked her to be his wife, however old-fashioned that might seem. To Pippa it was the ultimate compliment one partner could pay the other, the desire to be legally and emotionally bound together but this was not the time to articulate such an opinion and she was surprised to discover that, in spite of her grandmother's recent advice that a wedding was the way to go, she had every intention of accepting Ian's invitation. It might not be a proposal of marriage, she reasoned, but surely that wouldn't be far behind if she played her cards right? Her gut reaction was to accept his offer, so brushing away the disappointment that had been lurking at the back of her mind, Pippa didn't keep him waiting any longer and finding her voice again and picking her words very carefully, she finally gave him the positive reply he so desperately wanted.

"I had been hoping you would ask me to move in with you sometime," she said quite truthfully, "And the answer is 'yes' because I would love to, but I'd just like to know what brought this on all of a sudden. Why now?"

Ian's face revealed his relief and delight and at once it broke into a smile.

"It wasn't sudden for me. I have been mulling it over for ages and I had it all planned," he explained. "Then Ivy got ill and it brought me up short. It reminded me that no one knows what the future holds for them nor what is lurking round the corner and I just knew without the shadow of a doubt that you moving in with me was what I wanted more than anything else in the world. It also made me realise even more that I'd like to make the most of our time together. I'm not really bothered about reducing our carbon footprint Pippa, I just want to share my life with you," he added simply and earnestly.

Pippa thought that she should respond, but her mind was still taking in the awesome fact that Ian wanted to share his life with her and before she could find the appropriate words he added, "Actually there's something else. Hang on a minute," and he reached into his pocket to retrieve the shiny new key. Ian then took hold of her hand gently and placing the key in her upturned palm, he closed her fingers over it very carefully.

Pippa felt a lump forming in her throat but she held the key tight, swallowed hard and a nanosecond later, having regained her composure she said, "Thank you Ian, you *are* a dark horse," and then she added with endearing candour, "I may not have had a clue that you wanted me to move in with you right now, but I feel I should warn you that I am not a very tidy person and I can be a bit bossy sometimes."

"Did you think I hadn't noticed?" said Ian with a laugh and he took hold of her hand again.

"I love you just the way you are," he said gently, looking at her in a way that made her heart melt and all her reservations disappear.

"I would just like to add that I've been wanting to ask you to move in with me since as far back as Valentine's Day, but I couldn't pluck up the courage until now. I haven't told anyone about this yet, so it's going to come as quite a surprise to some people."

"I suppose you mean Mike," she said astutely. "Let's keep it like that for a while. At least until I've moved some of my stuff in."

"Your table is ready now," said a waiter who had sidled up to their seats unnoticed by the love-struck couple.

"Thank you, we're just coming," said Ian.

"Our new arrangement will solve another little problem too you know," he said to Pippa as they both stood up ready to walk over to their table.

"And what might that be?" Pippa asked.

"I won't have to buy any new pictures after all, because we can use the ones from your flat," he said audaciously.

"I knew it," said Pippa stifling a giggle, but pretending to be upset. "You only wanted me for my mother's paintings."

"Got it in one," laughed Ian happily, putting a protective arm around her shoulders as they moved across to eat.

15

Sunday morning found Ian and Pippa waking up to their new life together. Pippa had decided that she would have one more night at her flat to think about what she needed to take with her and on Saturday afternoon, after their visit to Ivy in hospital, Ian had collected the boxes she had packed and they had driven in convoy to his house.

They had decided to break the news to Mike and Gaynor at lunchtime, as the old Sunday lunch arrangement had not yet as yet been kicked into touch and Pippa was planning to tell her parents and Tim some time after that.

"We will have to do some more decorating you know Ian," she said, looking round the kitchen as they ate their breakfast.

"Yes, I know. Part of my cunning plan for getting you to move in was so that you could help me with it," said Ian, still on cloud nine. "Can I hear your phone ringing?"

"Oops, I left it upstairs," said Pippa and she raced off to fetch it. "It was Dad. He has left a message for me to ring him back. You don't mind, do you?" said Pippa walking back into the kitchen a few moments later with her phone in her hand.

"Go ahead, I'm going to do the washing up," said Ian.

"That's something we need in here when we do up the kitchen," said Pippa with a smile. "A great big dishwasher." Ian threw a tea towel in her general direction, but Pippa had skipped neatly out of range and was now selecting her parents' number on her phone. Fortunately it was her father who answered her call.

"Hello Dad, I have just picked up a message from you."

"Good morning Pippa, thank you for calling me back so soon. I'm ringing to let you know that your mother and I are coming down to Linchester on Tuesday. We are staying at Roman Reach for a few days, my birthday present to her actually and I wondered if you and Ian would be free to join us for dinner there on Thursday." Then a slightly worrying thought occurred to him and he added quickly, "You hadn't forgotten about Mum's birthday, had you?"

"Of course not Dad," declared Pippa indignantly. "That's a super idea, I'm sure it will be fine. Does Mum know?"

"Oh yes. I couldn't possibly arrange a trip without her say-so, you know what she is like. She's not too happy about putting the dogs in kennels though, but it would be very difficult to bring them with us and she did not want to miss this opportunity of seeing both of you and Tim of course, so we have agreed a compromise. We are dropping them off at Will Grace's place on the way down as a matter of fact and picking them up again as soon as we get back. We are both looking forward to seeing everyone again." Pippa was making faces at Ian while she was listening to her father, to see if she could let him know about their new living arrangements. Eventually the penny dropped and Ian nodded his head enthusiastically.

"That's good, Dad. I have something to tell you too, as it happens," she said and then went on in a very straightforward fashion, "I have moved in with Ian and I'm going to rent out my flat."

"Have you indeed?" replied her father, only slightly surprised. "Well I can't say that it is unexpected news.

You have always been a very sensible girl and at your age you should know what you are doing. I'll tell your mother and I expect she will be on the phone as soon as she comes in from her walk. I'm going to ring Tim now. See you both soon," said Adrian and with that he signed off.

"What did he say?" Ian asked at once.

"He said he wasn't surprised and that I am a 'very sensible girl' and should know what I'm doing, but then he is a man of few words. I expect Mum will have a lot more to say when he gives her the news. She might have been a fan of flower power in the sixties, but she is a bit more straight-laced these days. Anyway, they are coming down here next week and Dad wants us to join them for dinner on Mum's birthday. I said we could go, I hope that's all right," she said, suddenly realising that she had rather taken Ian for granted.

"What day is it," he asked.

"Thursday, I mean the fifteenth, that is next Thursday, no I mean *this* Thursday," said Pippa getting flustered.

"I *think* I'm free, let me just check my diary," teased Ian. "Yes I'm sure I am. Where are we eating?"

"Roman Reach, do you know it?

"I do and it is very smart. I'll have to get my suit out of mothballs *again*," he said seriously. "That will be the second time in as many weeks." Pippa's face was a picture. Surely he didn't use those smelly things? She would have to check in the wardrobe before she unpacked her clothes.

"I'm only joking," he said cheerfully, hazarding a guess at her unspoken thoughts. "Don't you think you should get dressed now? Silk pyjamas are not quite the thing for Sunday lunch."

Eventually both of them impeccably turned out, Ian and Pippa arrived at Mike and Gaynor's house just before half past twelve. Ian knocked on the door and it was opened shortly afterwards by a young woman in her twenties, casually dressed in baggy blue jeans and a pink long-sleeved tee shirt with a high neck and 'gorgeous' printed across the front. She had very short dark hair and was wearing a large cross hanging from a leather thong around her neck. She looked rather like Ian himself, which wasn't surprising seeing as the young woman standing on the threshold was his eldest niece, Jane.

"Hello Jane, I didn't know you were at home," said Ian, giving her a big hug, which was warmly reciprocated.

"Hi Uncle Ian, I'm here to do some revision. My exams are in a couple of weeks and I needed somewhere quiet to work, with food on tap," she explained with a smile, then looking at Pippa, she added in a friendly way, "You must be Pippa, nice to meet you."

"Hello to you too," said Pippa in reply.

"Sorry," said Ian contritely, "I had forgotten that you two haven't met."

"I recognised Pippa from one of Dad's photos," said Jane as they all traipsed out of the sunny March afternoon and in through the front door on their way to the sitting room.

"Pippa, Ian, how are you doing?" Mike said cheerfully as he walked into the room behind them. "What can I get you to drink?"

"We're fine thanks, Mike," said Ian, beginning to feel a bit nervous about letting the cat out of the bag, particularly to his brother. "I'll just have an orange juice if that's all right. How about you Pippa?"

"Mineral water please," said Pippa politely.

"Are you both on the wagon? I'm going to have a glass of wine. Are you sure I can't tempt you," he said, waving a bottle of Chianti at them.

"No thanks, I might have one later though," said Ian. "I can smell roast lamb, where's the chef?"

"She's just putting the finishing touches to her lemon meringue pie," said Jane, "I'll go and get her."

"At least the weather is a bit better today, isn't it? I hope it stays dry for a while now or that site is going to be a mud bath," said Mike. "How did the auction go on Friday?"

"Not bad," said Pippa. "Gran's bowl did very well, but not quite as well as your mum's jug," she added.

"Good, good," said Mike, thinking that Ian was a bit quiet and wondering if he was quite well.

"Hello everyone," said Gaynor, who had just materialised from the kitchen. "I hope you're all hungry because I'm roasting an enormous leg of lamb."

"Jane said you've made a lemon meringue," said Pippa eagerly. "It's one of my favourite puddings."

"Mine too," said Jane joining in. "Is lunch nearly ready Mum, I'm starving."

"Almost. You can go and sit at the table if you like, I'll be with you in a minute," said Gaynor before she retreated back into the kitchen.

Mike led the way, followed by Pippa, then his daughter and finally Ian, who was thinking he would broadcast his news when they were all sitting down and the meal was served, until then he would keep as low a profile as possible.

As the last golden roast potato dropped off Gaynor's serving spoon and onto her dinner plate, Ian judged that the time was right, so he took a deep breath and then launched in with his revelation.

"Pippa and I have something to tell you," he said, glancing at each friendly face in turn to check they were listening. Time stood still for a moment and Mike paused, a fork full of lamb halfway to his mouth. Four pairs of eyes homed in on Ian.

"Pippa and I," he repeated, "Have moved in together."

Mike's fork clattered down onto his plate along with the aborted mouthful of lamb which was left in disarray right next to the generous helping of cabbage, matchsticks of carrot and a crispy mound of Gaynor's delicious roast potatoes. Jane did not bat an eyelid and under the table, Gaynor trod on Mike's foot, while at the same time smiling at Ian and Pippa in turn and saying mildly, "Have you? When did all this happen?" realising with a pang of regret as she said it, that the smart new outfit in her mind's eye would not be seeing the light of day after all.

"Well, yesterday actually. Pippa is going to rent out her flat for the time being. We decided it would make our lives less complicated."

"Yes, we spend so much time together now, having one base seems best," chipped in Pippa, thinking Ian could do with a bit of moral support.

Mike was trying to stop himself from asking why Ian had not asked the girl to marry him. This was all the wrong way round. What in heaven's name was the matter with his brother? He decided to have a word with him later but in the meantime he would get back to Gaynor's tasty lunch and try not to rock the boat, fortunately remembering for once that discretion was the better part of valour, which might have had something to do with him having had his little toe severely squashed by his affectionate wife.

Lunch was finished in due course, helped along the way in part by Jane and her university anecdotes plus, just for Pippa's benefit, some grisly tales from the gap year she had spent out in Africa as a volunteer. As soon as he had the opportunity, Mike invited Ian to go outside with him to inspect his latest purchase, which was a new state of the art filter for his fishpond and as they walked into the garden together, Mike wasted no time in voicing his thoughts.

"What's all this about, Ian? Why haven't you asked Pippa to marry you? You seem very fond of each other and I know it's none of my business, but I think you should make this living together a bit more proper. A ring on her finger, that's what you need," he said rather abruptly.

"Thanks for the advice, Mike," said Ian in a controlled voice, trying not to get too hot under the collar at his brother's interference, "But this *is* two thousand and seven and I *am* over eighteen. I'm not quite sure yet what Pippa's views are about marriage, but when I've worked that out and if she's keen for a wedding *then* I will ask her; I don't want to rush it and frighten her off you know. Anyway I'm not discussing it now, but I will promise to let you and Gaynor know if or when there are any further developments."

Mike, recognising the subliminal message of 'mind your own business I know exactly what I am doing', should have decided to back off. However, although he had said his piece and didn't want the situation to escalate into bad feeling on both sides now he and Ian were working together, he felt very strongly instead that he should just add one more comment.

"You've obviously thought about it carefully mate, I'll give you that, but I still say you should do the right thing and ask her to marry you. Isn't she worth it?" he asked in a confrontational manner.

Ian was starting to feel downright annoyed at Mike's attitude and it showed in his face. So much so that even Mike understood that he was treading on very dicey ground and he then, it has to be said somewhat reluctantly, had the good sense to say, "All right, all right, I won't say another word. It's your life after all," and swiftly changed the subject to let things cool down. "Did you see Ivy yesterday? Gaynor and I are popping in this evening to give Claire a break."

"Yes, she was propped up in bed when I saw her," said Ian, glad that the topic of conversation had moved on. "She managed to talk for a bit, but she is still very weak. I'm going again tomorrow. It just shows you that none of us knows what fate has in store for us and I have come to realise that we should make the most of what we've got," he said pointedly, drawing a large black line under any more discussion.

"Quite right. Ivy is a tough old bird though and I expect she'll be up and about before you know it," said Mike appreciating the logic in Ian's last comment if not completely agreeing with the way he was going about it.

"Well, they were decidedly underwhelmed," said Ian as he and Pippa drove home together.

"Yes, I suppose they were a bit surprised," replied Pippa. "It doesn't matter what they think, does it? We are happy together and that's what counts," was her prosaic conclusion.

"Mike tried to interfere as usual, I'm sure he thinks I'm still a teenager. In his revered opinion he thinks that we should be getting married," said Ian, testing the water.

Pippa's heart beat a little faster, but she managed to answer him calmly and sensibly with, "Marriage is all very well, but these days a wedding costs a lot of money if you want to do it properly, so you have to be very sure it's what you want."

It was a non-committal reply, leaving the question wide open for him to interpret as he saw fit. Pippa did not want him to think she was desperate to be a bride, even though had he asked her to marry him at that precise moment she would have given him a resounding 'YES'.

Ian said nothing but inside he was feeling quietly elated. Pippa wasn't against marriage per se and his master plan was right on track.

16

Tim returned from his holiday on Sunday evening to find several interesting messages on his answerphone, but the one from his father took priority and he called him back as soon as he'd put his bag down and gathered his thoughts. The telephone only rang briefly before Adrian answered it and Tim launched straight in with, "Hello Dad, sorry I wasn't here when you rang. I've only just got back from the airport."

"It's good to hear your voice Tim, I'm glad you are back safe and sound. No broken bones I hope?"

"No, we've had a great time. Fortunately it's only the bank that's broken," joked his son. Adrian laughed and then explained why he had left the message on Tim's phone.

"I rang to say we're coming down to Linchester on Tuesday, it's a birthday trip for your Mum. Will you be free on Thursday night? We would like you to join us for a meal at Roman Reach."

"Wow! That's a bit pricey, Dad," said Tim.

"Yes, well it *is* Mum's birthday you know. Are you free or not? Pippa and Ian are both coming and your mother is looking forward to having all the family together for once."

"No pressure then," quipped Tim and then sensing his father's impatience, he decided to give him a sensible reply.

"Yes, I'll be there. I'm glad Ian is coming too, he seems like a good sort of bloke and his friend has been helping me with recording some of my music," said Tim.

"As it happens, I know all about that," said Adrian, happy now that his plan seemed to be coming together nicely, "Pippa told us when she came up to see us. Can you be at Roman Reach for seven thirty on Thursday?"

"I expect so," said Tim and they carried on chatting for some time, including a discussion of the state of the snow in France and reminiscences of family holidays on the piste.

The second call Tim made was to Garth whose phone was on answerphone, so all Tim could do was leave him a message to say that he was now back home and keen to have the latest news on his CD. Finally he rang Pippa but unfortunately call number three was not a great success either as Pippa seemed to have her mobile phone switched off. There was no reply from her landline either, which of course was not at all surprising because she was not even in the flat, but being ignorant of this fact Tim promised himself that he would try again later. It was just as well anyway, he thought to himself, as Pippa would be bound to keep him chatting for ages and he still had his unpacking to deal with and a mountain of washing to sort out too.

His sister, as it happened, had other fish to fry. She had gone up into Ian's attic with him to see if she could help him decide what else he could turf out, but she wasn't enjoying herself very much as it was quite gloomy up there and Pippa's one concession to being highly strung was an irrational fear of spiders. She hadn't mentioned this to Ian because she wanted him to carry on thinking of her as a together sort of a person, but she knew the truth would emerge eventually and the longer she stayed in the attic, the more likelihood there was of it being sooner rather than later.

"It's quite dark up here Ian, I hope I don't trip over something or put my foot through one of your ceilings," she said in a slightly anxious tone.

"They are *our* ceilings now," said Ian happily putting Pippa straight and thinking to himself how nice it was to use the plural possessive pronoun and not to be restricted to the singular 'my' any longer.

"Well, is there anything up here we could chuck out? Clearing out junk is very liberating you know," he said cheerfully, "I was quite pleased with the job I made of the garage, I threw away such a lot of rubbish that I've even got room to put a car in there now," he finished with a smile, remembering the sense of satisfaction he had achieved when the garage was finally empty.

"I could do with a torch," said Pippa, still trying to stifle the butterflies that were flapping about in her stomach, while she got down on her hands and knees to look through some old books. "And it's freezing up here. There's a tremendous draught coming from somewhere," she complained, giving her arms a vigorous rub with the dual purpose of trying to warm herself up and also frighten off any marauding arachnids. "What are you going to do with the pile of books downstairs?" Pippa asked, hoping this question would give Ian the excellent notion that perhaps leaving the attic to sort them out instead was a good idea.

"I haven't decided yet," he said and then picking up on the latent anxiety in her voice he added, "Do you think we should go and have a look through them now? They are rather in the way in the hall. Perhaps that would be more useful than trying to make some headway up here, there's so much to do and it *is* getting late. We could come back and have another go when I've fixed up some better lighting system."

Bingo, thought Pippa and she was up off the floor, brushing down the cobwebs from her skirt and heading for the loft ladder before Ian had time to catch his breath.

"Good idea," she said, just her head above the parapet now. "A cup of tea would be good too, all the dust has made my throat a bit dry."

Downstairs once again, a tremendously relieved Pippa sat on the floor in the hall and started to look through all the books Ian had piled up against the wall when he had emptied the bookcase that had been sold at auction the time before last.

There was nothing very startling amongst the volumes, no rare first editions or valuable antiquities, but as she picked up Ian's copy of *The Lord of the Rings* a piece of paper fluttered out and on to the carpet beside her feet.

Pippa picked it up. It seemed to be a note addressed to Ian dated May 1985 and signed by someone called Nick Rudge.

"What's this all about Ian?" Pippa called through to the kitchen where Ian was just pouring out two mugs of tea. He looked bewildered as she held up the small piece of paper for him to see.

"I don't know," he said walking towards her and putting the mugs down on the hall table. "Let me see," he added, the hint of a frown clouding his brow. He took the note from Pippa's hand and read it through twice and then the light dawned at last.

"Oh yes, I remember now," he said the frown melting away, "I was given that at the stage door of one of the concerts Garth and I went to. The tickets must have been a birthday treat judging from the date on the note. We were very cheeky in those days you know and always tried to get autographs if we could. Nick was the roadie for 'The Slight'. They were a local heavy rock group, do you remember them? I don't think they lasted long." Pippa shook her head and he carried on with his explanation. "Garth's cousin knew Nick and said he would get their autographs for us, but it turned out to be Nick's autograph that he ended up with and not the ones of the group after all. We were both rather hacked off when he handed that over, but then I suppose Nick Rudge thought he was just as important at the time. I have a whole pile of other autographs somewhere, probably in the attic. Shall I go and have a look?"

"No," said Pippa abruptly, which made Ian look at her with a rather startled expression, then realising she might have given herself away, she added calmly, "Why don't we go and sit in *our* lounge and drink our tea? I've finished here. I think you should ask Jane or Susie if they would like some of these books and if not, take them to Oxfam."

"Are you all right, Pippa?" Ian asked as they both sat down to drink their tea, wondering if he had done something to annoy her. Pippa decided that enough was enough and she would have to explain, so feeling a tad foolish, she told him of her phobia.

"There, you see," she concluded, "I am not as sensible as you thought I was, am I?"

"Is that all?" Ian replied, much relieved. "I thought it was something I'd done to annoy you. Lots of people are frightened of spiders Pippa, it's nothing to be ashamed of. I quite like them myself, but I do understand," he said kindly. "I know, I'll bring all the bits and pieces down from the attic some time and put them in the spare room and we can go through them there instead, but not this evening, don't worry. I'll do it one day when you are out at work. Anyway, thanks for going through the books, I had thought of asking Jane and Susie if they wanted some of them, myself. I think I might keep one or two of them and then ditch the rest like you said, because Mike never reads books and he hasn't got a sentimental bone in his body, so he wouldn't want to keep them just because they belonged to my parents."

Then he said as an afterthought, "You really should have told me Pippa."

"I know, but I didn't want you to think I was making a fuss about nothing," she said, snuggling up to him on the settee.

"I wouldn't have thought that at all. As I've told you before," said Ian staunchly, "I love you just the way you are."

17

The days were now dragging for Ivy, whose improvement had been maintained steadily; so much so that the doctors were even talking about discharging her the coming weekend but only if she went to stay with her daughter for a few days which Ivy was having trouble accepting, the more like her old self she became.

Ivy relished her own space and always had. She had never quite hit it off with Claire's husband either, but if it was the only way she was going to be released from the straightjacket of hospital routines, then so be it.

Ian and Pippa had visited her nearly every day and she always enjoyed their company. She was in complete agreement with Gaynor (who had also been a regular visitor, with and without Mike) and although she didn't know it, with all the rest of both their families too, in hoping that Ian and Pippa would get married soon as she very much wanted to see the ceremony take place and she had just had an unpleasant reminder of her own mortality. Her recent bout of pneumonia had been a wake-up call. She decided that if she got Ian on his own she would have a chat with him about it and see if she could hurry things along a bit.

For Isobel and Adrian, the contrary was true. Their stay at Roman Reach was going far too fast and Thursday was upon them without so much as a by your leave. Isobel woke up on her birthday to find that Adrian was already up and about and had left a card beside the bed for her to read. She could hear him having a shower in the en suite bathroom, so she sat up in bed, opened the envelope and read her first birthday card of the day, which is where Adrian found her when he came back into the room about five minutes later.

"A very happy birthday, darling," he said effusively and gave her a big kiss. "Have you decided what you would like to do today?"

"Oh thank you and thank you for the card Adrian, it's lovely. We-e-ll," she said slowly, "I would quite like to visit that new art gallery that has just been opened in Linchester and perhaps we could have some lunch at one of those little pubs on the way down to the coast. What do you think darling?"

"That all sounds eminently achievable," said Adrian. "I didn't order breakfast in bed as I know you like to eat in the dining room and I don't want to hurry you, but it is already half past eight." Isobel couldn't believe it. She never stayed in bed this late at home but, she rationalised to herself, it was her birthday after all.

That evening, Ian and Pippa arrived at Roman Reach at the same time as Tim, Pippa carefully carrying the present for Isobel, now tastefully wrapped up in some stylish glossy brown paper which was tied up with raffia and neatly finished off with a tightly knotted double bow.

"Hello Tim," she said and gave him a quick hug.

"Hello, its ages since I've seen you," was his friendly reply. "And hello to you too, Ian. I have been trying to ring you Pippa. Are you never at home these days?" Pippa looked at Ian, who smiled back at her but said nothing. He thought he would leave Pippa to tell her brother their news. She certainly didn't need his help.

"Funny you should say that actually," she started, "You're right, I'm not in my flat much now, probably because I have moved in with Ian," she said with a grin, then she stopped to see what Tim would make of her news. Tim, it has to be said, was caught completely unawares by this news, but being the consummate lawyer he was, he managed to keep his cool and just said diplomatically, "Have you?" whilst wondering what he should say next.

Ian decided that it was time for him to enter the arena, so he said quickly, "You must come round one evening and have supper. I'm sure Pippa will give you the address later and fix up a date when we are all free. We have some catching up to do about lots of things, including your music. Oh, look Pippa," he added, "I think I can see your parents sitting over there."

Adrian had seen them all come in and was standing up, beckoning them over. He thought Pippa looked lovely in her long skirt, green cashmere sweater, grey suede jacket and grey high-heeled boots and that she and Ian made a fine couple. He was constantly surprised at how tall his son had now become and pride swelled in his chest for his family. Isobel's feelings closely mirrored her husband's, but she was too busy kissing everyone to register them at that precise moment and then her attention was taken up with unwrapping her birthday gifts.

"Happy birthday, Mum," said Pippa as she handed over the carefully wrapped parcel to Isobel. "I hope you like this, it's from both of us."

"Thank you both, then," laughed a delighted Isobel. "It is so good to see you again so soon, and to see you too Tim. We haven't seen you since Christmas I don't think. We have been having a really decadent few days here, it's been lovely," said Isobel trying to undo her gift.

"The best thing for me has been the excellent real ale they serve here," said Adrian unexpectedly.

"Really? I like a good beer myself," said Ian pleased that he had at last found something he and Adrian had in common.

"Have you tried Summer Lightning? I can thoroughly recommend it," he said, but unluckily his comment fell on barren ground, due to the fact that Isobel had now succeeded in getting into her parcel by slipping off the raffia at one corner and she was holding up the robe for all to see.

"This is absolutely gorgeous, Pippa. Where on earth did you find it?"

"It was in the auction actually and as soon as I saw it I knew I had to get it for you. I'm so glad you like it."

"I love it," said Isobel, her eyes sparkling.

"Here is my effort Mum. Not quite so stunning, but something else I hope you'll like," said Tim with a smile.

"Now, what have we here?" Isobel asked putting down the exotic robe and taking a small parcel from Tim's outstretched hand.

Tim's gift for his mother, which Isobel discovered a few minutes later was a bottle of her favourite expensive French perfume, had been brought back from his recent skiing holiday in France and Isobel was equally delighted with his choice for her and said so immediately.

She felt truly blessed that she had two such thoughtful and generous children and that her equally thoughtful husband had arranged this trip for her so that they could all be together on her birthday. These thoughts instigated yet another round of hugging and kissing until Adrian called the meeting to order.

"Right, now to the serious business of eating," he declared. "What is everyone having?"

As the meal drew to a successful conclusion, Isobel and Pippa retired to the cloakroom and Isobel, taking advantage of getting her daughter alone for a change, tried to find out what her future plans might be with regard to Ian.

"What exactly is happening with you and Ian?" she asked as soon as the cloakroom door closed silently behind them.

"We've got a lot of decorating and updating to deal with in the house and the attic needs rationalising too," said Pippa, wilfully misunderstanding her mother's question.

"That wasn't what I meant and you know it," said Isobel a little sharply, still hoping Pippa might discuss the 'M' word with her voluntarily.

"Well if you mean marriage, Ian hasn't asked me and I'm certainly not going to ask him," said Pippa defiantly, then taking a deep breath she added calmly, "Look Mum, we are just enjoying being together at the moment and getting used to being a couple. What do you think of my new boots? Ian bought them for me last week. I think he was getting a bit tired of seeing the black ones all the time," said Pippa hitching up her skirt a fraction and displaying the boots for her mother to admire, hoping to deflect her from the unwanted topic of conversation but Isobel, she was to discover, hadn't quite finished.

"They are very smart Pippa but it's no good changing the subject," she replied, not taking the hint. "I read in my Sunday newspaper only last week that cohabiting couples feel less tied to a relationship than married ones and are apparently more prone to something called, now what was that expression?" Isobel asked herself, a frown appearing on her usually smooth brow.

"Oh yes, 'rapid euphoria and rapid burnout syndrome' I think it was. Don't get me wrong, Pippa, I like Ian, but love on its own is not enough. Once you have rented out your flat and signed the lease, what will happen if you fall out with him? You will have nowhere to go. It's a bit precarious setting up home with someone after only knowing them for such a very short time and without the insurance of a wedding ring and a bit of commitment. I know I'm unconventional, but even in my wilder days I would never have countenanced such an idea. I just hope you both know what you are doing," she said. "I'm very concerned about this you know Pippa; I do wish we lived a bit nearer."

Pippa knew that when her mother started going on a bit and used lots of long words, she had to take cover, so instead of retaliating she said in clipped tones, "Yes I know," whilst at the same time thinking that at that precise moment, Isobel was just a tad *too* near.

She made up her mind there and then not to tell Ian anything about this conversation that she heartily wished she was *not* having with her mother. Didn't Isobel realise that Pippa, as a sensible person, had weighed up all the pros and cons of moving in with Ian? Ian had complained that his brother thought he was still a teenager, well in her mother's case, thought Pippa, Isobel still looked upon her as a little girl and not the grown woman she had become. How annoying was that?

It might not have been so galling if she did not in principle agree with a lot of the points her mother had made. She really wanted Ian to ask her to marry him and she had only settled for second best because she loved him so much and trusted him implicitly. To be fair, her mother did not know Ian like she did and although Pippa felt a bit guilty for not wanting to discuss the ins and outs of her relationship with her mother at this point, she also realised that if he finally did get round to proposing, Isobel would be the first to know.

In an effort to put an end to any more of her mother's intrusive comments, Pippa decided on a diplomatic retreat and excusing herself somewhat frostily, she went off to sort out her hair. The repetitive action of running the brush through it over and over again proved very therapeutic and eventually calmed her down.

Isobel for her part was now satisfied that she had got her point across and she had nothing further to say. She was prepared to rely on Pippa's innate good sense to do the rest and she felt sure her message would eventually sink in. Consequently, when Pippa was ready to return to the rest of the party, albeit still smarting from her mother's criticism and very keen to avoid a repeat performance and she made one last effort to change the subject, she finally succeeded.

"I forgot to ask you earlier," she said making a valiant attempt at a smile as they approached the table once more. "How is Dollie getting on?"

"Who on earth is Dollie?" asked Tim intrigued, catching the tail end of their conversation.

"A dog that thinks she's a cat," quipped Adrian.

"What?"

"I think your Dad means she is a very lucky little dog who, had she been a cat, would have used up one of her nine lives," said Ian thinking he was helping.

"Now I'm really confused," said Tim. Isobel took pity on her son and explained all about Dollie and her brush with death and Ian and Pippa's part in her rescue and then finished by telling Pippa how the puppies were getting on.

"We saw them when we left Nip and Tuck at the farm on the way down here. They are very sturdy little things for only three weeks old. Will has put Dollie and the puppies in an outhouse for the moment so they can't come to any harm."

"Is he going to keep them all?" Ian asked her.

"I don't know, he didn't say, but I shouldn't think so. They already have several farm dogs and Dollie is just the children's pet," she said.

"Will you two be in any time tomorrow?" Adrian asked his daughter. "I thought your Mum and I could pop in on our way home."

"I could be there at lunchtime," said Pippa a bit doubtfully. "What about you Ian?" she asked, willing him to say that he could too. There was no way she wanted to be alone with her parents at the moment. She held her breath and crossed her fingers behind her back.

"Yes, I'm sure I could too. We could organise some lunch for you if you like," he said eagerly. Pippa's shoulders relaxed and she gave Ian a very grateful smile. Ian noticed the smile and thought Pippa must have had one glass of wine too many, but he smiled back nevertheless, pleased that everything was turning out so well and, as he was completely unaware of Isobel's concern for her daughter's security of tenure, feeling quite at home in the bosom of the Flynn family.

18

It was a week later that Pippa was sitting in the Cathedral tearooms waiting for her friend Alice, to join her for lunch. Alice was an air hostess on long haul flights and her work schedule could be somewhat erratic, so Pippa hadn't seen her for some time. Eventually, they had found a day that would suit them both and this was it. She had so much to tell Alice that she didn't know if an hour would be long enough to get it all off her chest, but as Ian had so wittily suggested, she would just have to talk very fast.

The tearooms looked out over a walled garden in the Cathedral precincts and were bright, airy and attractive. They worked like clockwork with an efficient waitress service and there was constant coming and going. This particular lunchtime, it was very busy and the flock of customers seated at little round tables covered in bright gingham cloths, seemed like humanoid gannets settled on their cliff-top retreat, some with their heads nodding up and down in animated chatter or others with their knives and forks duelling over the food artistically presented on shiny white shell-like plates. There was a continuous low-grade babble of many and various voices, interspersed with the occasional swooshing of the espresso machine by the till as the roaring waves of steam came gushing out of it.

Alice appeared at the door of the tearooms in due course, looking eye-catchingly elegant in a short-skirted suit in the latest shade of green, with a pink linen scarf draped tastefully around her neck and shoulders. Unlike Pippa, Alice had short fair hair and eyes that were an unusual shade of pale blue which verged on aquamarine. Pippa noticed her at once and waved across the multitude of bobbing heads to attract her friend's attention.

This had the desired effect and Alice came straight over, closely followed by a waitress who had been alerted by Pippa to the fact that she was waiting for her companion before she ordered lunch.

"At last we meet," said Alice comically. "You are looking incredibly good Pippa. What's your secret?"

"Imperial Leather?" said Pippa with more than a touch of irony, quite ready for her friend's good-humoured banter. "It is really good to see you Alice. Let's order our food and then I can tell you all my news and you can tell me all yours," said Pippa happily. They gave the waitress their orders and started on the debriefing. It was, to begin with, rather one-sided because Pippa was keen to let Alice know everything that had happened to her, from Valentine's Day onwards. Alice knew about Ian of course, but she had no idea the relationship had galloped on so fast and Pippa's tale had her transfixed as it came across to her as so heart-warming and romantic.

"I am absolutely delighted for you, Pippa and I can't wait to meet your gorgeous man," she said between mouthfuls of her Waldorf salad and sips of water. "It's a bonus that he gets on so well with your family. My father can't stand Simon, which makes life a bit tricky at family gatherings, but fortunately as Dad lives in France we don't see him too often and my mother worships the ground Simon walks on, which more than makes up for my peculiar father." Pippa laughed. She had almost forgotten how amusing and forthright her friend could be and it felt good to be in her company again even if it was only for one very precious lunch hour.

"So what's been happening to you? I have hogged the limelight for long enough," said Pippa.

"Well, I do have some rather good news myself," said Alice with a dazzling smile which immediately gave Pippa the idea that some momentous beans were about to be spilled and after a slight pause during which her friend's imagination was working overtime, Alice said with a hint of triumph in her voice, "Actually, I'm pregnant."

"*You're what?*" Pippa squeaked, dumbfounded.

"Expecting a baby, in an interesting condition, big with child, what more can I say? I'm a bit disappointed that you're not pleased to hear my news Pippa," said Alice, a twinkle in her eye.

"I *am* delighted for you, of course I am, but you love your job. You have never, ever, hinted at becoming a mum. How on earth did it happen?"

"Well if you don't know at your age, I'm not telling you," said Alice with a happy laugh. "I suppose my body clock was ticking. I'm a couple of years older than you, you know and I am truly weary of living out of a suitcase when flights get grounded or there are airport strikes. I suppose you could say I'm ready to settle down now and so is Simon. He is taking early retirement from the airline and is looking into the possibility of setting up a business teaching people how to fly so that he can have more regular hours too."

"When is the baby due?" asked a still incredulous Pippa. Alice had always seemed to her to be the last person in the world to want a family. How wrong could she have been?

"Well, I am just four months pregnant and my due date is the 22 August, I *think,* or round about then anyway. We didn't want anyone to know about this until we were absolutely sure everything was OK, you can never tell at our age, can you? It has been really hard not to mention anything when we have talked on the phone though, so I am glad you know now."

Pippa at last came to her senses and congratulated Alice properly. Her lunch break was nearly over and she was due back in the office for a meeting, so she couldn't sneak another few minutes to carry on chatting, but they happily agreed that when Alice had finally given up work, they would be able to meet a lot more often and keep in touch more easily.

"I will ring you when I am finally earthbound and perhaps you can introduce me to Ian at last," said Alice, "But if there are any further developments with you two in the meantime, I want to know straight away," she finished with a smile.

"Don't hold your breath," said Pippa, dryly. "We are very happy as we are at the moment, despite the disapproval of my mother and Ian's brother about our living arrangements." Alice pulled a sympathetic face and after exchanging a hasty hug, the two friends went their separate ways, Pippa heading back to work.

She couldn't get her head around Alice having a baby. She had a mental picture of Alice in her stewardess's uniform, hat perched at a jaunty angle on her head, wheeling a trolley down the high street with one hand whilst balancing a tray of bottles on the other, her baby neatly strapped to her chest. This was obviously going to take some getting used to.

Ian was back home just before Pippa and had made a start on their evening meal when she walked in through the door.

"Hello, did you have a good day?" he asked, turning round to give her a kiss.

"Not bad. I had a big surprise at lunchtime though, Alice told me she is pregnant," said Pippa, picking absent-mindedly at some carrots he had just chopped up and was about to put in a saucepan full of water.

"I love babies," said Ian somewhat unexpectedly. "When Jane and Susie were born I was always round at their house to help out. In fact, you are in the presence of a highly-experienced baby sitter you know."

"Am I indeed," said Pippa her mouth full of carrots. "Strange as it may seem, I have never had much to do with babies and I'm always put off with the amount of noise they make; I never quite know what it is they want, which worries me."

"Food, a cuddle or a clean bottom usually," said Ian with a chuckle. "Does this mean we are not going to have any little Pippas or Ians running around under our feet then?" he asked, a strange expression on his face.

"Oh, I do hope so at some stage," said Pippa enthusiastically. "Babies are a bit unnerving, but I just *love* children."

This was music to Ian's ears and the last piece of the jigsaw he needed to complete his research programme.

Pippa of course, her sixth sense having it would seem taken an inconvenient sabbatical, knew nothing of this and went off to lay the table oblivious to the fact that her last innocent remark had sealed her fate as far as a marriage proposal from Ian was concerned.

Their meal over, Ian and Pippa were sitting in the lounge, discussing their plans for the house.

"You know that paint you wanted for the kitchen?" Ian began, "Well, Mike has ordered it and the painters can be here next week," he said and then suddenly remembering something else he had to tell her, he added, "Also, I have brought home some brochures of floor and wall tiles for you to look through and if we can make a decision on those too, perhaps we can go and get them tomorrow while we are out and about. Mike has told me the best warehouse to go to. I think I left them on the coffee table," he said and he went over to fetch the information for her to see.

"You have been busy Ian. I can't wait to have the kitchen spruced up a bit, then we can have a go at the bathroom. I've been looking round a few showrooms on my travels and I think I have an idea of what you might like," said Pippa, keen for Ian to know that she was doing her bit too.

"Good. Oh yes, I forgot to mention that Claire rang me earlier to say that Ivy would be home this evening, so I thought I would pop round and check that she is all right if you don't mind."

"No, you go Ian. I'll look through these leaflets and shortlist a few I like," said Pippa, flicking through the pages of one of the brochures as she spoke. "I was thinking we could have it all done while I am off work over Easter so that I can keep an eye on things."

"Good plan," said Ian and left Pippa to her exploration of the world of tiles.

Ivy eased herself into her favourite armchair with a satisfied sigh. It was good to be home. To be fair, the short stay at her daughter's house had not, after all, been as bad as she had thought it might have been and although she tired easily and still had a persistent cough, she felt very much better in herself. She just wanted everything to return to normal now, so she sipped her cup of tea and checked her newspaper to see if there was a good detective yarn that she could watch on the television before she went up to bed.

No such luck and Ivy didn't think she had the stomach for watching a hospital series, having just diced with death herself, nor did she relish the idea of being shown how someone else could clean up their disgustingly filthy house, so when she heard Ian's key in her lock, she was very pleased indeed.

"Hello Mrs E., it's only me," he called, not wanting to startle her.

"I'm in here Ian," she replied obliquely but Ian, having seen the light from outside the house as he walked up the drive, knew he would find her in her sitting room and made his way there without further ado.

"It's good to see you home again," he said, walking over to her chair and giving her an affectionate hug and then sitting down on a small but comfortable television chair placed conveniently opposite hers.

"I am very relieved to be here, believe me," she said with a rueful smile. "I did think a few times in hospital that my number was up, but it seems the powers that be have other ideas."

"You are looking very much better now anyway. Claire said she had stocked you up with food, so you won't have to go out for a few days and if you need anything at all, just ring Pippa or me," he said helpfully.

"Oh yes," said Ivy, sitting bolt upright in her chair and giving him a steely stare. "I had forgotten. You two are living together now aren't you? I wanted to talk to you about that." Ian was a little taken aback, but he just smiled politely and waited calmly for her next comment.

"What have you got against marriage? You of all people are not afraid of a bit of commitment, as you proved when you looked after your mother so well, so it can't be that. Perhaps you haven't even asked Pippa? Surely you weren't scared she would turn you down? I have seen the way she looks at you and if I'm not very much mistaken, she would accept your proposal in a flash." Ivy was pulling no punches as usual and having said her bit, she sat back to await Ian's response.

Ian was used to Ivy and her straightforward ways. He admired her honesty and as her comments happened to come just after he had made up his own mind about what to do, he decided to give her an honest answer back.

"I will let you into a little secret Mrs E., but only if you promise not to breathe a word of it to anyone, not even the vicar." Ivy was all ears and nodded her head to indicate that she accepted his terms.

"Well, I *am* going to ask Pippa to marry me and very soon too, but I'm not going to tell you how, where or exactly when, so you will just have to wait and see."

Ivy beamed broadly at Ian and leant over towards him to pat his arm enthusiastically.

"I knew it. I knew you would do the right thing. Good boy, your Mum would be proud of you. I promise not to say anything but don't forget to let me know when it's all out in the open, will you?"

Ian promised she would be one of the first people to be told and, satisfied that she had everything she needed, he let himself out and went back to Pippa and her fact-finding mission.

19

The following two weeks passed very quickly for Ian and Pippa but by the end of them the kitchen had been painted a delicate shade of blue which contrasted nicely with the pine cupboards and the floor and wall tiles had been chosen and bought. They were now languishing in sturdy boxes in the garage waiting for Mike's men to come over and put them in situ.

Auction day was nearly upon Pippa yet again, but on the Thursday before, she had an unexpected telephone call from her mother.

"Hello, Pippa how's the decorating going?"

"Fine thanks, Mum," said Pippa, trying to sound cheerful but with a sinking heart, expecting another diatribe from her mother about the pitfalls of living together without being married.

"We are just waiting for the tiling to be done now. The men are pencilled in for Monday unless Mike has an emergency somewhere else," she ended brightly.

"That's good," said Isobel, her daughter's domestic arrangements being the last thing on her mind at that minute. "I was just wondering if you had got round to renting your flat out yet?"

"Not yet, why?" Pippa asked, bristling and wondering what was coming next.

"Well, sadly Dad's old cousin Bert died yesterday," she began. "If you remember, he lived in Littlehampton and Dad and I would like to come down for the funeral next Wednesday so we thought that if the flat were available, perhaps we could borrow it for a couple of nights and then Nip and Tuck could come with us," said Isobel, her fingers firmly crossed, hoping that she would not be tempted to reveal her hidden agenda to her daughter.

"Oh dear, poor Bert. I only have a hazy recollection of him. Is Dad very upset?" Pippa asked, concerned for her father but at the same time much relieved that she wasn't in for another dose of her mother's admonitions.

"Not really. He was ninety-four after all. So, is the flat available at the moment?"

"I don't see why not," said Pippa quickly thinking that she would have to go over to the flat at the weekend to tidy it up a bit before her parents arrived.

"That's great. Thank you so much sweetie. It will literally be just the two nights because we have some friends coming to see us over the Easter weekend," said Isobel, very satisfied that her arrangements had been so easily made.

"Why don't you come round for supper on Tuesday night?" asked Pippa, thinking that this would be an ideal opportunity to prove to her mother once and for all that she and Ian were very happy and settled together. "I'm on holiday next week and I'll have plenty of time to make a decent meal for you both if you'd like that," she said hopefully and she was very pleased when Isobel accepted her offer.

She had stuck to her guns and had not mentioned their awkward conversation at Roman Reach to Ian, especially after the reaction Ian had got from his brother, because she was a little embarrassed by her mother's trenchant attitude and she didn't want Ian to feel pressured into proposing, much as she wanted him to. They were getting on really well together as they were and she didn't want their bubble to burst.

"We *can* stay at the flat," called Isobel to Adrian who was regulating his bracket clock in the sitting room.

"Humph!" replied her husband, knowing exactly what she had in mind and wishing that she hadn't.

"I hope you didn't have another go at Pippa while you were on the phone," he said, sounding rather edgy.

"No, I did not. I've had my say, for all the good it did. I couldn't get any sense out of her then and I don't suppose much has changed in a couple of weeks. I can lecture her as much as I like but ultimately she is a grown woman who will make her own choices, even though to me she will always be my baby girl and I can't help worrying about her," said Isobel and then she added gleefully, "I do so hope they like my little surprise Adrian."

Adrian sighed and shrugged his shoulders. Sometimes he despaired of his wife and her 'little surprises'. Goodness knows what Ian and Pippa would make of it.

And so it was that after a weekend of feverish activity, at six o'clock on Tuesday evening Pippa was calmly working her culinary magic over a roast chicken, eagerly awaiting the arrival of her parents.

"Shall I open some wine?" Ian asked her helpfully, having already changed out of his work clothes into a pair of chinos and a casual blue shirt which, she noticed, made his eyes look a deep and very attractive sapphire blue.

"Yes, please," said Pippa, "I put a bottle of rosé in the fridge earlier." Then she added thoughtfully, "You know, Ian, I could get used to this housewife malarkey. It rather suits me." Ian smiled enigmatically to himself, but did not reply.

"I am going to see if they have arrived yet," said Pippa, but just as she was about to peep through the blinds in the sitting room to have a look outside, the doorbell rang, so she rushed off to open the door instead, with Ian in hot pursuit.

"Hello Mum, Dad," she said happily ushering them inside and kissing them both on each cheek, then noticing that her mother did not have any hangers on in tow, she asked, "Where are the dogs?"

"We stopped for them to have a run on the way here, so they will be quite happy in the car for a bit," said Isobel smiling sweetly.

"How was the journey?" Ian asked Adrian as they walked through into the lounge.

"Not too bad considering it is Easter this weekend," replied Adrian. "By the way, Isobel has got you a housewarming present and I want you both to know it wasn't my idea," he said a trifle apologetically.

"That's kind of you Mum," said Pippa, thinking it must be one of her mother's abstract paintings if her father wanted nothing to do with it because he had no taste for modern art.

"You have spoilt the surprise now darling," said Isobel, not unduly put out. "I suppose I had better go and fetch it then," she added and she disappeared out to the car again, returning not long afterwards with a small cardboard carrier in her hand.

Ian and Pippa were mystified until they heard a tiny scrabbling noise coming from inside the box. Whatever Isobel had brought them, it was not an abstract painting.

"Before you look in the box," said Isobel, "I want you to know that I have thought long and hard about this and if you really don't want my gift, we'll take it back to Hardale with us."

"For heaven's sake," said Pippa, getting slightly impatient at all the procrastination and keen to see what exactly was in the carrier. "What *is* it?"

Ian thought he knew and Adrian's next comment as Isobel handed the box to Pippa, confirmed his suspicions.

"You know, I shouldn't have described it as a 'house *warming* present'," he said with wry humour. "The expression 'house *wetting* present' would have been more apt."

Pippa carefully opened the box and had to put her hand over her mouth to stifle a squeal of delight so as not to scare the puppy, for puppy it definitely was.

"Ian look," she said, her eyes shining, "It's a sweet little puppy."

When the dust had settled a bit and the puppy was sitting on Ian's lap, looking up at him adoringly, while he stroked her soft brown ears, Isobel explained how the puppy had come to be a housewarming present. Apparently Will Grace had telephoned the Flynns to explain that he had found homes for the other two puppies, but this little one had no takers and he wondered if Ian and Pippa might like her after all the trouble they had gone to, to rescue her mother.

"I couldn't say no, could I?" Isobel finished, appealing to their better natures if such an appeal were necessary.

"Mum, Ian has always wanted a dog and you know I love dogs too. I'm happy to keep her and as I'm on holiday at the moment and the tiles are safely down on the kitchen floor, it gives me a good opportunity to settle her in. I bet you're not going to say no, are you Ian?"

"Certainly not," said Ian stoutly, "And what's more, I can tell you what we're going to call her too. It has to be 'Millie' after the waterfall that nearly finished her off."

"You see," said Isobel smugly to her husband as they set off for Pippa's flat at the end of a very enjoyable evening, "I knew they would love her."

"All right, all right, I should have trusted your judgment," said Adrian as he negotiated his car out of the gate. "I must say they seem very settled there."

"Yes, it won't be long now," said Isobel enigmatically.

"What do you mean darling?"

"I mean, my love, that I didn't have to worry after all and if I were one for reading the tealeaves, I would be seeing our daughter walking down the aisle on the arm of that very handsome Ian Chisholm."

Millie settled down fairly quickly for such a small puppy and soon discovered the delights of Ian's shoes which seemed to exude an irresistible scent, not to mention the attraction of anything at floor level which she considered fair game and excellent for cutting her teeth on. Pippa soon learned not to leave bags of shopping on the floor if Millie was awake and each time Ian came in from work he seemed to have brought yet another squeaky toy with him. He was counting the hours until the Easter weekend so that he would have four whole days to spend with Pippa (and the puppy of course) and the time to play out the final act of his carefully choreographed proposal scene.

"I think we should have a day out tomorrow," said Ian out of the blue on Good Friday afternoon as he and Pippa were eating their lunch.

"But what about Millie? We can't leave her here on her own all day, it wouldn't be fair," said Pippa looking at the little bundle curled up in what seemed to be a rather oversized basket, now with untidy ragged edges as Millie had decided to give them a very good chew. "I think we should stay here and do a bit of gardening. Actually I've been thinking that a conservatory might be nice along the back of the house. Perhaps we could nip out to the garden centre and look at a few designs while Millie is having a nap."

"We could do that," said Ian slowly, thinking on his feet. "But I'd rather go out with you for the day. There is plenty of time for gardening and yes, I do like the idea of a conservatory, but I suggest we speak to Mike first to check on planning rules and so on. Anyway," he said brightly, "I thought Ivy might like to come round and puppy sit."

"Well, I suppose that would be all right," said Pippa slowly coming round to the notion of having a day out. "You could pop round and ask her. Where are we going anyway?"

"I thought we could drive down to Portsmouth. It's ages since I've been, I don't know about you. I would like to go up the Spinnaker Tower, then we can have some lunch, do a bit of shopping and get a takeaway for our supper."

"That sounds like fun," she said, finally won over. "You know shopping and eating out are two of my favourite things and the Spinnaker Tower is a bonus, but we can't go unless Ivy can help us out, so you'd better get round next door quick."

Ian didn't need any more encouragement and headed for Ivy's house with a big grin on his face. He thought Ivy could easily be persuaded to help out, especially as Ian and Pippa now had a new thirty-two inch flat screen television in their sitting room and a fine collection of *Midsomer Murders* DVDs.

He hadn't taken Ivy's key on this occasion because she was very much better now and had regained enough energy to get around her house and garden quite well, so he rang her bell and waited. The door opened in due course and Ivy appeared resplendent in a bright yellow silk jersey dress, two rows of colourful trading beads round her neck and some rather smart blue and red shoes on her feet, which confirmed Ian's view that she was practically back to her old self and probably up for a bit of puppy sitting.

"Hello love," she said good-naturedly. "Come in. What can I do for you?" Ian followed her inside, patting Hiawatha irreverently on its head as he passed the big wooden statue standing in the hall.

"Pippa and I would like to go out for the day tomorrow, but we don't want to leave Millie on her own all day so we wondered if you would come over to do a bit of puppy sitting for us," he said optimistically, placing all his cards on the table straight away.

Ivy looked at him closely, carefully considering his request and then she said, "Have you got anything good for me to watch while I'm there?"

"How about some *Midsomer Murders*?" Ian asked, knowing that she would find this offer too tempting to resist.

"Just down my street Ian, first class, I love John Nettles. What time do you want me?" Ivy replied predictably and without any hesitation.

"How does ten o'clock suit you? We should be back by five I should think," said Ian.

"Consider me in," she said cheerfully and Ian went back home to give Pippa the good news.

20

Easter Saturday dawned fresh and bright, which augured well for their day out and Ivy turned up promptly at ten o'clock as arranged. Millie found her capacious handbag very tempting and lost no time in snuffling around it with avid interest. She had just removed a packet of mints from it, when Pippa noticed what she was up to and quickly retrieved them before the puppy got so much as a lick.

"Don't leave anything on the floor Ivy or Millie will be after it, she is full of mischief," warned Pippa

"No!" said a doting Ivy. "She is a little sweetheart," and Millie, quickly realising that Ivy was a pushover, sidled up to her, her tail wagging like a metronome set on 'vivace', yapping her approval.

"Well, we had better be off," said Ian. "Pippa has left you a sandwich in the fridge and you know where the tea is, don't you?"

"Of course I do. Off you go, both of you, Millie and I will be fine," said Ivy and settled herself down in front of the television, an acolyte by her side.

Ian and Pippa set off for their day out in high spirits.

"I tried to get up the Spinnaker Tower when it first opened, but there was some hiccup with the lifts and I haven't tried since," said Pippa.

"I never got round to it, but I've heard the views are spectacular on a good day. I'm glad it's not cloudy today, we should be able to see for miles," said Ian in reply. They chatted on happily, discussing things they had or hadn't done in their lives and then Pippa asked, "Have you thought any more about your new car?"

"Actually, I have," he said. "I've been doing some research and I think I'm going to settle for a Saab convertible. I thought if you agree, we might call in at the Saab showroom later on as we go right past the door on the way back and book a test drive."

"It's a good job we set off early then," laughed Pippa, delighted that Ian wanted to make the most of their day together.

Eventually having parked the car in the vast multi-storey car park, Ian and Pippa walked through to the entrance at the base of the Tower. The place was humming, with shoppers scurrying here and there criss-crossing the walkways, each one laden with bulging carrier bags, some with children in tow. The street traders were selling cut-price jewellery, artworks and sticky sweets and there was a generally good-natured, holiday atmosphere throughout the complex.

They bought their tickets and a view book and then waited in the queue for a lift to take them part of the way up the one hundred and seventy metre high structure.

"It says here that the views stretch out over twenty-three miles," said Ian informatively, noting from the booklet with his engineer's eye, that the spire section alone was twenty-seven metres long.

"It's amazing how they got it all to stand up straight," said Pippa in astonishment. As the lift rose slowly up the tower, Ian noted another interesting fact, which he eagerly imparted to Pippa.

"Did you know that it is actually visible from aircraft flying at thirty thousand feet? Incredible. And it is constructed from the seabed on piles," he added. Pippa was amused at his incredulity, but she too was very impressed with the Tower and couldn't wait to get right to the top to check out the view. Ian, however, had not quite finished marvelling at this 'must see' attraction.

"What's more," he added in amazement, "The amount of structural steel they used, weighed as much as *twelve* blue whales, can you believe it?"

Pippa agreed that it was all very surprising, but she was more interested in trying to identify any landmarks she could see through the windows.

As they arrived at the top platform, after a final climb up a small flight of stairs, a splendid panorama was spread out in front of them. They could see right across Portsmouth dockyard and as far as the Isle of Wight beyond.

There were only two other people on the top platform with them and after a very short while they left to go back down again and Ian knew without a shadow of a doubt that this was *the* moment. He waited for a few minutes to gather his thoughts, letting the wind at the top of the Tower push him a bit nearer to Pippa.

"Just look at all that sea," enthused Pippa. "I feel like the monarch of all I survey."

"Well, I can't give you all of that," said Ian contemplatively, "But I was hoping to ... give you myself."

"What on earth do you mean?" Pippa said with a laugh, thinking he was joking and she carried on checking out the view.

"Philippa Flynn," said Ian very formally, "Would you do me the honour of becoming my wife?"

Pippa turned round and looked at him standing beside her, a very serious yet tender look on his face, but she seemed to have been deprived of speech.

"Pippa," he said in exasperation, "Help me out a bit here. I am asking you to marry me." Then, thinking he realised what had been lacking, he dropped on one knee and repeated firmly and clearly, "Pippa, will you marry me?" Whilst registering the fact that he wanted to keep this picture of her standing at the top of the Tower, her burnished hair in disarray, her green eyes luminous with unshed tears, in his mind's eye forever.

"Ian Chisholm," she said, picking up on his formal tone, all thoughts of the view now entirely expunged from her brain, "I would be honoured."

Ian only needed telling once and he was up on his feet in a flash and enfolding her in a warm embrace, which lasted for a good few minutes until they heard the next party of sightseers arriving.

"I haven't quite finished yet," said Ian, slowly disentangling himself from her arms. "I haven't bought you a ring because I want you to choose your own. I'm hoping you will be wearing it for many years to come and I didn't want to saddle you with something you really didn't like, so-o-o I came to the shopping centre a couple of days ago to one of the jewellery shops downstairs and picked out three rings I liked, that I thought you might like. They've put the rings to one side for you and now you can go and make the choice yourself. Are you ready to come?" What a foolish question. Pippa was *more* than ready and she left Ian in no doubt as to that fact. She couldn't stop herself from smiling but, nevertheless, she managed to reply eagerly, "Of course I'm coming, I can't wait to see what you've chosen."

Ian had found it very difficult to pick out three rings that he thought might appeal to Pippa. He definitely wanted diamonds to come into it somewhere because, after all, diamonds are forever, but he wasn't sure if the shank should be traditional yellow gold, or stylish platinum. The final winners were one square emerald with two smaller diamonds set on either side of it in yellow gold, a sapphire and diamond cluster in yellow gold and a traditional diamond solitaire set in platinum.

Pippa felt like a child left alone in a sweet shop; she didn't know where to start, or which delicacy to sample first. The extraordinary thing was that all the rings fitted her perfectly so she just had to decide whether she wanted a coloured stone or not. Ian was not prepared to influence her decision in any way and he even made matters more difficult for her by saying that if she didn't like the ones he had picked out, she could choose another one altogether.

An hour later and Pippa had finally made her choice and they had left the shop together hand in hand.

"Shall we go and find some lunch?" suggested a very contented Ian. "I'm glad you chose that one because it was my favourite," he said, taking hold of her left hand to scrutinise the ring.

"Oh, you know me so well," said his fiancée with a smile. "Who shall we tell first?"

"We're not going to tell anyone until I have had something to eat," said Ian firmly, "Come on, I've booked a table at the Italian restaurant round the corner."

"You never cease to surprise me," laughed Pippa. "And to think I didn't want to come out at first. How long have you been organising today?"

"About three weeks I think. It's been quite hard not to leave any clues lying about you know and when Millie turned up, that made things even harder because until I hit upon the idea of Ivy looking after her for the day, I wasn't quite sure how things would pan out."

"Well, as far as I'm concerned, every detail has been perfect," said Pippa fiddling with her new ring and looking like the cat who had got the cream. Then, tucking the hand with its precious adornment safely inside the crook of Ian's arm as they strolled round to the restaurant together, she added, "Even down to the weather, I wonder how you managed *that,*" and finally, whilst smiling up into his face which reflected back the warmth of her gaze, she remarked, "I think I'm going to like being Mrs Chisholm."

21

They lingered so long over their lunch that it was nearly four o'clock before they left the restaurant. A trip to the car showrooms was now out of the question, but they managed a quick stroll round the quay instead and then set off for home.

"Can I ring Mum now? I'm bursting to tell someone that I am an engaged person," said Pippa, still riding high on a wave of elation.

"Go ahead. Do you think she will be surprised?"

"I don't know," she said thinking to herself that her mother would be ecstatic, never mind surprised, if their recent tête-à-tête was anything to go by, "I'll …." and she didn't have time to finish her sentence with 'find out in a minute' as her father had answered the phone.

"Hello Dad,"

"Hello back," quipped her father, obviously in a good mood. "This is a nice surprise."

"I've got a better one for you, Ian and I are engaged," said Pippa excitedly. "We're going to get married," she added, just for good measure in case her father hadn't understood the word 'engaged'.

"Oh Pippa, how wonderful. Hang on a minute, I'll call Mum." Pippa could hear her father shouting to Isobel to pick up the phone, then after a few seconds her mother's voice came on the line.

"Hello Pippa. What have you just said to your father? He is looking a bit peculiar."

"Only that Ian and I are engaged," said her daughter triumphantly.

"Pippa! Sweetie! That's marvellous news, how exciting. Congratulations. Has Ian bought you a ring?

Tell me all about everything," said her mother, absolutely thrilled with this turn of events.

Pippa explained about their trip up the Spinnaker Tower and Ian's proposal and her mother listened attentively without interrupting once, but as soon as Pippa had finished, Isobel asked her a very strange and seemingly irrelevant question.

"What does this Tower look like?"

"Well, like a gigantic steel sail I suppose. Why?"

"Of course," said Isobel, not immediately answering the question. "*That's* what Gran saw in your tealeaves. She said something to do with masts or boats. What she *actually* saw was the Spinnaker Tower," she concluded, very pleased with her powers of deduction.

"How weird," said a very surprised Pippa, "Maybe there's something in Gran's psychic powers after all, or it could just be a coincidence as we live near the coast," she added, her innate common sense floating to the top once more. "Don't you want me to describe my ring?"

"Of course I do," said her mother eagerly.

"Well," began Pippa, looking admiringly at her left hand, "It's a beautiful platinum diamond solitaire."

"It sounds fantastic. When are you coming up to show us?"

"I can't say yet, Mum, but very soon I hope."

"Well, I am absolutely over the moon for you. Do you want me to tell Gran?"

"No thanks. I'm going to ring her right now," said Pippa.

"I won't spoil the surprise, then. Oh yes, before you go, how's that little Millie doing?" Isobel asked.

"She's fine Mum, chewing everything in sight though," said Pippa and then left her delighted mother to discuss the exciting news with her equally delighted father but she might have been a bit put out, had she heard their subsequent conversation which went something like this.

"I hate to do it," began Isobel gleefully.

"Yes, but you are going to anyway," replied Adrian with a resigned smile.

"I certainly am," said his wife, "I told you so."

Pippa had no luck contacting her grandmother, as Edith was at an Easter Bonnet Parade in the village, but she managed to catch Tim who, on hearing about the engagement, was touchingly pleased for his big sister and wished them both well. They arrived back home to find that Ivy and Millie were both fine and that there had been no mishaps while they had been away. Now it was Ian's turn to broadcast their momentous news.

"Have you had a good day?" Ivy asked them. She was settled comfortably in an armchair with Millie lying stretched out across her knees.

"Yes, excellent," he said and then hesitated slightly. "Erm, we have some news for you, Mrs E." Ivy was all ears and she shuffled expectantly in her seat wondering if this was the news she had been waiting to hear for so long.

"Pippa and I are engaged," said Ian, hoping that she wouldn't let slip that she had already had an inkling of this news beforehand, but Ivy was not going to let him down and she got up out of her chair quicker than she had been able to for many months, giving Millie a nasty shock and tipping the little dog over onto a cushion, leaving her legs and tail in disarray.

"That's marvellous news," she said, her old face wreathed in such a big smile that her eyes practically disappeared amongst her wrinkles. "I'm so pleased for both of you, I have been hoping this would happen for ages," she said and she walked across to the happy couple to give them both a hearty hug. "I hope I will be invited to the wedding. When will it be?"

"We wouldn't *dare* leave you out," said Ian with a laugh, "But give us a chance, we've only just got engaged. How about joining us for a fish and chip supper to celebrate?"

"Definitely," she said enthusiastically. "Cod and chips for me."

22

The next day was of course Easter Sunday and Ian and Pippa had been invited to Mike and Gaynor's for the first barbecue of the year, weather permitting. Mike was renowned for his sumptuous barbecued food, especially his spare ribs and vegetable kebabs, so they were really looking forward to going, especially as they could take Millie with them and Susie and Jane were both at home for the holidays which was an added bonus.

Fortunately the sun had decided to make a return visit and although the sky wasn't completely cloudless, there was no wind and it felt unseasonably warm outside, so it augured well for their al fresco meal. In the car on the way there, Ian and Pippa were discussing how Mike would take their news.

"Well, considering that he thought we should have been married before we even moved in together, I expect he will be very pleased," said Ian, "And I also expect that Susie will ask if she can be your bridesmaid," he added with a contented sigh.

"Yes, I have to consider all of that," replied Pippa thoughtfully. "Who *should* I ask to be my bridesmaid, or should I have more than one? When do *you* think we should have the wedding? And where?" Pippa asked him ruminatively. "What a lot of decisions we have to make."

"As far as I'm concerned, we could get married tomorrow, just you and me," said Ian gallantly.

"Well, it will have to be a church wedding I think, or I wouldn't feel quite married," said Pippa, wondering to herself if Ian would agree to the wedding being held at the little church in Hardale. "And I'm sorry, but I couldn't have the ceremony without my family there too. I haven't told you this before Ian, because with one thing and another it slipped my mind, but you know that briefcase Gran gave me when we called at her house?" Ian nodded as he stopped the car in Mike's drive. "It was full of sketches of wedding dresses she had designed herself and I promised her I would use one of the designs if I ever got married," she said and then a disconcerting thought crossed her mind.

"Oh no," she exclaimed, suddenly remembering that she hadn't actually told her grandmother what was going on. She hoped against hope that her mother hadn't let the cat out of the bag.

"What's wrong?" Ian asked her, a concerned expression on his face.

"I didn't try Gran again, so she hasn't heard the news. At least not from me. If Mum tells her first, she will be upset, I just know it."

"Right," said Ian, briefly checking his watch, "Do it right away before we get out of the car; she should be back from church by now."

Pippa didn't need any more encouragement and she quickly called up her grandmother's number. As usual, it took Edith a while to answer the phone, but when she finally picked it up, Pippa didn't waste any time putting her in the very romantic picture.

"Pippa, lovey, I knew it," she cried triumphantly. "What took you both so long?"

"I had to wait for Ian to ask me of course and don't worry Gran, I haven't forgotten my promise and I *have* got that diamond on my finger," said Pippa all aglow.

Edith laughed and told Pippa how delighted she was several times over and then honour having been satisfied, Pippa left her grandmother to mull over the news, with a reassurance that she would be in touch again very soon.

"Perhaps we could have a look at those designs together when we get back," said Ian getting out of the car and on seeing smoke rising from the back garden he commented, "It looks as if Mike has started already."

Pippa scooped up Millie from the back seat of the car and followed Ian through the side gate of the house, down a narrow passageway and out into the beautifully landscaped garden with its vast expanse of well-manicured lawn. The brick-built barbecue was just beyond some decking which spanned the width of the house and sheltered by a trellis fence that had ivy and honeysuckle creeping all over it, the tendrils curling in and out of the diamond shaped voids making a very efficient windbreak. Mike was standing there, surrounded by trays of uncooked food, waiting for the coals on the barbecue to reach their optimum heat, wearing a plastic coated apron with a voluptuous female torso in a skimpy red bikini printed on the front of it over a pair of blue Bermuda shorts and a Linchester Wanderers tee shirt.

Gaynor had laid the garden table with colourful plastic plates and tumblers and was just coming out through the back door with a jug full of Pimm's when she saw Ian and Pippa strolling round the corner.

"Hello you two, let me just put this jug down, then I will come and meet Millie," she said with a welcoming smile and she called to her daughters who were still languishing in the sitting room reading the Sunday supplements, "Susie, Jane, come out here and see your Uncle Ian and Pippa." Mike heard her call and turned round.

"Oh good, you two have arrived at just the right time. I am about to put everything on the barbecue," he said.

The clouds of smoke heralding the barbecue had now dispersed with the help of a light breeze that had sprung up. It was ruffling the serviettes Gaynor had placed artistically in the tumblers on the table and Millie's nose was twitching madly because the same breeze was carrying the mouth-watering scent of uncooked beefburgers and sausages right over to her, tantalising her olfactory nerves and making her wriggle in Pippa's arms, but Pippa had her in an iron grip and had no intention of letting her break free and run riot.

Gaynor, having put the jug down on the table, walked across to stroke Millie at which point Susie and Jane both materialised from the house and were drawn to do the same thing; Mike of course was too engrossed with the job in hand to join them and having placed a neat row of sausages to sizzle appetisingly on the wire rack over the smouldering charcoal, he stayed exactly where he was a large pair of tongs at the ready.

"Could you come over here for a minute, Mike," called Ian, girding his mental loins for the big announcement, "I have something to tell you." Pippa had been hiding her left hand under Millie up until now, but when Mike joined them she moved Millie onto her right arm and the sun caught her diamond and made it glint and sparkle sensationally. Gaynor saw the ring straight away, but apart from an involuntary sharp intake of breath, she did not reveal that she had noticed anything.

"Pippa and I got engaged yesterday," said Ian baldly as he watched Mike's face a little nervously. Jane and Susie shrieked in unison, immediately rushing towards Ian and smothering him in kisses, then they moved across to Pippa to give her the same treatment, which in turn encouraged Millie to add *her* accolade which consisted chiefly of a thorough and very vigorous licking of Pippa's face.

"Steady on girls," said Mike smiling benevolently. "Congratulations! Though not before time Ian," he said and shook his brother's hand warmly, then kissed Pippa on the cheek.

"Well done," said Gaynor, waiting her turn to congratulate the happy couple with yet more embracing. "I love your ring Pippa."

"Thank you," said Pippa, waving her hand about for them all to take a look.

"Well," blustered Mike, "What a beauty. You certainly won't need a torch to see in the dark when you're wearing that, will you?" which comment made his daughters dissolve into helpless giggles.

After all the excitement had died down and the barbecue was being devoured by all and sundry, including Millie who had been allowed a corner from Ian's beefburger, Mike and Ian managed to have a quiet word together.

"I've been waiting to say that I am really pleased for you, mate and I know you are both going to be very happy," said Mike. "You *look* very happy and so does Pippa, not to mention that little dog of yours. I told you ages ago that I had a good feeling about you two getting together," he added smugly.

"Thanks Mike. I really appreciate what you have done for me over the past few months," said Ian feeling a little self-conscious. "I did have something I wanted to ask you actually."

"Ask away, if I can I will," said Mike jovially.

"I was wondering if you would be my Best Man."

Mike, who was already as pleased as punch at the way things had turned out, felt as if his heart would burst. The request had come out of the blue and he was quite overcome that Ian had asked him to be his Best Man. Obviously the thought had crossed his mind and he would have *liked* to have been asked because in his opinion he was just the man for the job, but he had presumed Garth would have been granted that honour, being Ian's best friend.

"Gaye," he said, his cheeks flushed with pleasure, "Ian has asked me to be his Best Man. What do you think of that?"

"That's nice Mike. It's all so romantic, I simply *love* weddings," she enthused.

"But you haven't given me an answer," said a bemused Ian. "Will you do it for me or not?"

"Try and stop me," said Mike, still feeling like the cock of the walk. "It would be an honour."

"I know when we should get married Ian," piped up Pippa, having heard this exchange and being intoxicated with romance and a trifle too much Pimm's. "The seventh of the seventh, two thousand and seven."

"Of course," said her adoring fiancé, smiling broadly, "My lucky number."

❧❧❧